NOT LIKE I M

JEALOUS

OR ANYTHING

Not Like I'm Jealous

or Anything

The Jealousy Book

edited by marissa walsh

delacorte press

Published by Delacorte Press
an imprint of Random House Children's Books
a division of Random House, Inc.
New York

www.randomhouse.com/teens

Educators and librarians, for a variety of teaching tools,
visit us at www.randomhouse.com/teachers

Library of Congress Cataloging-in-Publication Data
Not like I'm jealous or anything : the jealousy book / edited by Marissa Walsh.
p. cm.
Summary: Thirteen writers share their visions of jealousy in short stories, essays,
and a poem.
ISBN 0-385-73317-8 (trade) — ISBN 0-385-90336-7 (Gibraltar lib. bdg.)
[1. Jealousy—Literary collections.] I. Walsh, Marissa.
PZ5.N658 2006
2005009095

The text of this book is set in 12-point Myriad Roman.

Printed in the United States of America

10 9 8 7 6 5 4 3 2 1

First Edition

BVG

For Steven and Joseph,
my nonrivalrous siblings

"O, beware, my lord, of jealousy; It is the green-ey'd monster which doth mock the meat it feeds on."
—Shakespeare

"Jealousy is in the house y'all, Fellas sing it . . ."
—Eminem

CONTENTS

JEALOUSY: AN INTRODUCTION
Marissa Walsh

I am a jealous person. It's one of my worst characteristics. But recognizing that you have a problem is the first step, right? So what am I jealous of? I'm jealous of people with TiVo. And iPods. I'm jealous of people who know what music I should be listening to before I do. I'm jealous of people who get to hang out all day and write, or paint, or tap dance, or do all three. I'm jealous of people who get to spend their summers on Cape Cod. I'm jealous of people who go on vacation to Italy. I'm jealous of skinny girls. With long flowing hair. Red hair—I'm jealous of people with red hair. I'm jealous of people who can afford Marc Jacobs. I'm jealous of people who aren't afraid to skydive. Okay—maybe not that. I'm jealous of people who've got it all figured out.

I suspected there were other writers (a notoriously jealous bunch) out there who felt the same way—or at least understood the way I feel. And I was right.

Reading the six short stories, four essays, one quiz, and one poem in this collection made me feel much better about my own green (and I don't mean recycling) tendencies. Face it, we may *say* "not like I'm *jealous* or anything," but as the title of one of the stories in this collection states so well, we're *all* green about something.

I THINK THEY GOT YOUR NUMBAH
Siobhan Adcock

It's hard to start without pushing off the wall. You feel
and smell other people's foot sweat. Gwen's rental
skates had still been hot and moist from the last user
when she put her feet into them. The roller rink had
not been Gwen's top choice. Even at ten, she was the
kind of girl who'd throw out the socks she wore to
roller rinks and bowling alleys rather than wear them
ever again. She had wanted to have a slumber party.
But she knew better than to want it, so she had pretended she didn't. She hadn't even mentioned it.

And now here she was with her friends, Kim, Kayla,
and Dawn, waiting out the pause between songs for
what would come next. Laura Branigan. Not for the
first time, either. Gwen and her friends shrieked and
clambered out of the food pit, abandoning their
nachos, struggling across the carpeted rest area, on
their way to swing around the smooth floor in oval
after oval. Gwen didn't even glance back at her
mother, whose only job today was to wait gamely on
a low carpeted bench in the food pit, watching other
people's kids roll past. Her mother's job today was to
make melted cheese appear on command, on anything Gwen and her friends wanted. She was to rent
lockers and keep track of the keys, so Gwen and her

friends didn't have to wad their coats up in a ball on a bench and hope nobody touched them. She was to wait in line to rent and return their skates. She was to stand by the railing and take pictures when Gwen and her friends got to do a solo skate, just for her party. Gwen and Kimmy were wearing matching polo shirts.

"Let's skate holding hands! All of us! Let's make a wall!" Kimmy shouted over *I think they got your num-bah*. Kimmy always had good ideas; she was a leader. They formed a wall. A singing wall. *I think they got the ALIAS!* They made their arms tense and formed a whip. *THAT YOU'VE BEEN LIVIN' UN-DAH!* Gwen was on the end that moved the fastest. She gave up the lyrics and screamed. Her friends whipped her even faster.

To be honest, it was the first time all day she'd felt as if she was enjoying herself. Gwen's mind had been on other things: Kimmy's vastly superior roller rink birthday party last month, with all the girls from their class; Kayla's slumber party on her birthday, back in January, with red velvet cupcakes and rented horror movies. Gwen was acutely aware of what her friends were thinking right now—but it was her own fault if they felt sorry for her.

Mostly Gwen had been thinking about her sisters, Avery and Sally, at home with their father on a cold Saturday afternoon. Sally, who was seven, had cried this morning because she couldn't come. Gwen, staring miserably at the living room carpet, had almost invited her. But then her mother had said (and this

2

was really what Gwen was still thinking about, even though she knew perfectly well what it meant): "Sally, baby, this is Gwen's special day with her friends. When your birthday comes we'll have a skating party for you. But Mommy can't bring you along today." Sally had cried even harder at that. She didn't get it.

Sally's tears were far from the only ones that had been shed over this party. Gwen had only been allowed to ask three girls. At first she had been stunned: she had raged, she had cried, and in the end she had been sent to her room in the middle of dinner, after her father had smacked her for being such a brat and for not appreciating how lucky she was to be having a goddamn party at all.

Her sister, Avery, who was twelve and prone to thinking that this made her wise, had found Gwen later, facedown on the lower bunk bed in the dark, seething. Gwen had been experimenting with screaming quietly into her pillow, a kind of high-pitched whistling keen that seemed to concentrate and focus the agony in her chest without actually relieving it much.

Avery didn't turn on the light. "Gwen. You okay?"

"Yeah." Still into the pillow. Hearing her sister's voice made Gwen start crying again. Avery sat down on the bed and put her hand on Gwen's back. Gwen didn't shake her off. (At the beginning of the school year, Gwen remembered, Avery hadn't been allowed to be a crossing guard, and all of her friends were. Avery had thrown herself on her bed and cried then, too, while Gwen had sat on the bottom bunk, feeling bad and strange. Their father had come in after a while, glanced sympathetically at Gwen in the bottom bunk, and stood next to the bunk bed patting Avery's back, just like Avery patted Gwen's now. Gwen remembered not being able to see her father's face, but his voice had sounded amused and kind: "I'm sorry, Avery. But it's not the end of the world, is it?")

"I have to tell you something important," Avery said, with her hand on Gwen's back.

"What." Gwen's face felt suddenly like it was burning off, a thousand tear-wet degrees of furious heat. She angled her head slightly to get some air on her skin without turning over.

"Mom's in the kitchen really sad right now."

"Good," Gwen said stormily.

"She wishes you could bring more people to the roller rink."

"Well, that makes two of us!" The hateful sarcasm was such an intense pleasure that it provoked a bitter, dorky-sounding laugh: *"Heuhh!"*

"I don't think Mom has the money to pay for more people."

Gwen started crying again.

"So don't be mad at her."

Gwen curled up in a ball and wept even harder. Avery sat with her for a few minutes. When Avery tried to pull a blanket over Gwen, Gwen kicked it off. "I'm wearing *shoes!*" she'd wailed. "Don't put my blanket on my *shoes!*" Avery got up and left, closing the door quietly behind her. Gwen hated when Avery acted motherish. She snarled after her sister in the dark: "Oooh, you're so *understanding!*"

Fury at Avery's goodness had sustained Gwen for about fifteen minutes, and then it transmuted into cold, tearless fury at her parents. She thought about pink cakes and ponies and streamers, and realized she'd never had that kind of party and never would. Never mind ponies—never *mind* ponies—she couldn't even have a freaking slumber party after what had happened at Avery's last year. And she definitely couldn't have a Pizza Palace party, like Dawn had had when she turned nine. Gwen knew that game tokens and pizzas and pop for fifteen kids cost a lot of money. Never mind Pizza Palace. She probably, Gwen thought, bitterness and envy burning a hole in her chest, couldn't even have a *Burger King* party, with stupid paper crowns and toys in little baggies. Gwen flopped on her bed in the dark most of that night, angry and staring and feeling crappy.

Which later, much later, once Gwen's heart rate had slowed, gave rise gradually to the crappiest realization of all: Gwen had treated her mother badly. She had made her mother feel bad.

Gwen thought of her mother crying in the kitchen—crying, Gwen thought miserably, about the very same thing she was in here crying about. Gwen hoped Avery had exaggerated. Avery probably *had* exaggerated—their mother never really cried—but that wasn't the point. Her father was actually right: she was lucky to be having a party at all. She was a brat. She was spoiled. The remorse was physically painful, as aching and pressurized as the bitterness had been. She had hurt her mother's feelings, and Ma was just trying to be nice. Gwen couldn't believe how awful she felt. And it was supposed to be her *birthday;* she was supposed to be *happy*! This thought made her miserable enough to cry all over again. The tragedy of it buckled her heart. Her mother tried so hard! They were so poor! Mom was so good! More tears at the thought. (But under the tears, shoved down where Gwen wouldn't have to look at them: pulsing, black jealousy and anger that her birthday party was still going to suck.)

When Gwen finally stopped crying, she felt heroic and weak, ready to admit her mistake, martyred and cleansed.

Gwen had crept into the living room before bedtime, red-eyed and sniffling. Her parents were reading and *The Honeymooners* was on the television. She was too ashamed to approach her father, who sat in his usual chair with an old yellow lamp shining on his book, and a few empty cans of Old Style at his elbow. Instead Gwen went to stand next to her mother, who sat with a paperback on the couch.

"Hi, baby." Her mother smiled at her.

"Hi, Mommy," Gwen whispered.

"Hey, poopy. Done sniveling?" her father asked jovially.

At which point Gwen found she was not done sniveling at all. Crying afresh (with snot, even), she managed, "I'm sorry I was a brat about the party!" And then she ran back to bed, sobbing.

So, tears and resentment. The roller rink party felt spoiled before it had even begun. Sally's tears this morning plus Gwen's tears for the last few weeks . . . Gwen wondered how much water it added up to. Enough to take a bath in, maybe. Gwen had even cried when it came time to invite people—not only that, she'd made *other* people cry. Her mother had told her she should ask her three guests privately, so no one would feel excluded, but the irony of it had made Gwen furious all over again, furious and mean. She had asked Kimmy, Kayla, and Dawn right in front of Casey, whom Gwen didn't like as much. (Gwen privately suspected Casey of trying to "take away" Kimmy, by which she meant Kimmy was her, Gwen's, best friend, and she should really act more like it and stop passing so many notes with Casey.) Casey had cried. Then Gwen had cried for being such a jerk, and apologized because she could only ask three people.

"Can't you beg your mom?" Kayla had asked woefully.

"No," Gwen had said. She thought about crying again. Then she stiffened up. She lifted her chin and looked at all of them defiantly. "My parents don't make as much money as yours do. I'm sorry."

It had impressed her friends (and soon, when the word spread, the rest of her class) more than she could ever have dreamed. The drama made her, somehow, briefly powerful. *Gwen's family is poor. But she's cool. She can only have three people at her birthday party— three people! But she never complains—you'd never know!* To Gwen's surprise, her noble suffering had given her a sudden and unprecedented prestige.

The minute Kimmy pulled a ten-dollar bill out of her pocket at the roller rink, though, Gwen would gladly have traded her prestige for a convenient hole in the floor to crawl into.

Her friends had brought their own money for snacks.

Nobody did that at someone else's birthday party.

"Mrs. Rodman? Would you like a pop?" Kimmy probably thought she was being polite. Gwen stared at the floor in horror, unable to meet her mother's eyes.

"Oh—no, that's very sweet of you, Kimmy, but I don't need one right now." Her mother sounded gracious and unsurprised. Gwen glanced at Dawn, who met her eyes. "There's cake and drinks on the way for you girls."

"Really? Thank you so much, Mrs. Rodman!" Kim said enthusiastically. Gwen felt her stomach wrench.

The cake and orange punch, as Kim knew perfectly well, were part of the birthday party package at the roller rink. It wasn't that big of a deal.

"Come on, Gwen, let's go to the bathroom," Dawn said suddenly, grabbing Gwen's hand.

You never went to the bathroom by yourself at the roller rink, unless you actually had to *go* to the bathroom. The bathroom was where you went with your friends to brush your hair and talk about your other friends and what they'd done to piss you off. As she and Dawn pushed off the bench to roll toward the girls' room, Gwen allowed herself a moment of satisfaction at Kimmy's expression.

There was a clot of older girls at the door to the bathroom, and Dawn and Gwen had to wade their way through carefully. Bumping into an older girl, even accidentally, could be a bad idea. Some older girls would go to the trouble of getting revenge if a girl Gwen's age nudged their elbow while they were touching up lip gloss or eye shadow. A classmate of Gwen's, Brianna, had spent most of Kimmy's birthday party hiding with Kimmy's mom in the food pit to avoid a gang of older girls. Brianna had bumped one of them into the sink in the girls' room, and the older girl and her friends had sweetly (*too* sweetly; they shouldn't have been trusted) forgiven her, and then pursued her with a grim, laughing mercilessness in the roller rink, circling her, yelling at her, pulling Brianna's hair and shirt, and even knocking her down once.

Dawn had Gwen's hand, and she maneuvered them to a spot between two mirrors. Dawn wasn't the prettiest of Gwen's friends—in fact, Dawn had thick black eyebrows and early braces—but she was matter-of-fact and she was loyal, and she was a total goof, so a lot of people liked her even though she still got teased. Gwen liked her. Kayla was prettier and Kimmy was funnier and more popular, but Dawn was the most like Gwen.

"Listen. I told her not to do that," Dawn said, frowning. "I told her it would just embarrass you. Kimmy's, like, a big actress sometimes. Which you know."

"Which we all know," Gwen agreed dryly.

The two of them leaned against the wall in thought for a moment. Gwen wondered if Dawn was remembering Kimmy's party. She was tired of people feeling sorry for her. She was tired of people feeling sorry in general.

"Dawn. What are you going to do for your birthday this year?"

"I don't know. It's not till April."

"Don't have a roller rink party. I think people are sick of coming here." Gwen flexed her toes in the tight skates and raised an eyebrow knowingly.

"I'm totally sick of having blisters."

"God. And I'm totally sick of that disgusting orange drink."

"And I'm sick and tired," Dawn lowered her voice, "of the tough girls here."

"I know. Me too. It's, like, trashy here. Dirty."

"But I don't think you should feel bad about having your party here," Dawn said quickly.

"I don't. I mean, it's fun to skate and stuff. And the nachos are soooo good." Gwen smiled, ready to change the subject.

"Gwen, don't mind me saying this. But it's actually a lot nicer being here with just the four of us." Dawn seemed very serious, and Gwen tried not to look surprised. One of Dawn's eyebrows had an orange fleck of Chee-to dust in it. "With a big party there's always somebody getting left out."

Gwen nodded. It was easy to become the left-out girl. Even Kayla had been the left-out girl once.

"So, this is more fun. It's more like a party," Dawn finished.

Gwen reached up and picked the Chee-to dust out of Dawn's eyebrow, showing it to Dawn on one fingertip, by way of explanation. But instead of laughing about the Chee-to dust, Gwen said, "Thanks for putting it like that."

"I mean it." Dawn shrugged.

"I know."

For Avery's birthday last year, her eleventh, Avery had had five friends over on a Friday night for lasagna and cake and a sleepover. Gwen and Sally had been allowed to sit in their pajamas and watch movies with the older girls, but only until nine-thirty. Gwen had watched her sister's friends lay out their sleeping bags in the living room, and while she and Sally sat on the couch, the older girls lolled around on the floor; the whole living room converted into a big soft nest. Avery didn't have a sleeping bag; she folded a comforter in half on the floor instead and put her pillow on it. Gwen's mother was in the kitchen at the table, reading and listening to the radio. Their father had gone out with friends after work that night, "to get away from all the females," as he put it. Gwen's father liked to complain about living in a house full of females, and she and her sisters often teased him about it. As he said, even the stupid cat was a girl. Gwen's mother had warned him not to come back too late. Or too drunk.

"We should pretend like the carpet's a moat and we can't walk on it, we can only walk on the sleeping bags," Sally had said, leaning against Gwen. "Like we're being chased by a monster, but we can't fall into the moat. Want to?"

"Shut *up*, Sally." Gwen wanted to sit—all the other girls were just sitting, they weren't playing around. Avery's friend Melissa had brought some of her mother's makeup; they were going to do makeovers and Gwen wanted to watch.

"Sally, come here," Avery's friend Denise said.

Sally obediently went to Denise on her sleeping bag.

"Can I do your hair? It's so long and pretty," Denise

said, smiling. Sally had fine, straight blond hair almost to her elbows. Gwen's hair was cropped into a Dorothy Hamill cut—not quite a bowl cut, but close enough. Gwen detested it. She knew she looked like a boy.

Gwen had to hand it to Sally, she played it very cool. Sally's eyes were shining with excitement, but she sat politely and calmly while Denise brushed her hair and braided it. Melissa looked at Avery and then said, "Gwen, do you want me to do your eyes?"

At nine-thirty Sally was summoned into the kitchen, with her head half-braided. "Time for bed, little girl," Ma said. From her seat on Melissa's sleeping bag, Gwen watched Sally beg for more time.

"But she's not done with my hair yet!"

"What, exactly, is being done to your hair?" Ma said, smiling, but looking curiously at Sally's multiple long braids—some looped, some hanging straight. "No, honey, I'm sorry. You have to go to bed. It's past your bedtime."

"Why doesn't Gwen have to go to bed?" Sally was upset. Gwen would have been upset, too, but she and her mother had already agreed that Gwen could stay up a little later with the girls if Avery would let her.

That was when the door had opened, banging against the wall, letting in a flying stream of wet cold air from outside. Melissa had actually screamed a little. Gwen's father lurched through the doorway.

"What is this, Invasion of Planet Preteen?" he'd

exclaimed cheerfully, slurring a bit. Avery's friends laughed.

But Avery did not laugh. Gwen had noticed. Gwen had looked at her older sister the minute their father came in the door. Avery sat on her folded comforter, back very straight, her hands in her lap, her face smooth with worry.

Sally came out of the kitchen with their mother then, and Gwen saw almost the same expression on her mother's face as she'd seen on Avery's—except her mother's worry was darker looking. Sally ran to her father, braids flying. She'd taken her first steps that way. The story was famous in their family: Sally as a baby, seeing her father come in the door after work, and being so excited that she stood right up and wobbled over to him.

"Sally, what the hell's wrong with your head?" Their father, a construction worker, was not a big man or a fat man or a particularly muscled man, but he was strong. He picked Sally up and stared at her in mock consternation. Avery's friends laughed even more loudly. "What have you preteen monsters done to my baby girl?"

"We were doing her hair, Mr. Rodman," Denise explained patiently, eyes twinkling. Denise was the most mature of Avery's friends.

"I can see that, smart-ass. But *what*," he said, staggering a bit with Sally in his arms, "were you doing with her hair?" He staggered a bit more, and Avery sat up on her knees, one hand stretched slightly forward. All the humor in the room seemed to fall into the floor in an instant. Gwen could see that Avery's friends were just now realizing that he was drunk—and they probably weren't sure a father should call his daughter's friends smart-asses, even as a joke. Gwen watched Melissa and Beth exchange a look.

Then her father lost his balance. Sally's legs slipped and her bare foot hit the side table. "Daddy!" Sally yelped. The lamp shivered.

"Paulie!" Gwen's mother was quick. She got her arms under Sally's bottom and scooped her away, *oof*-ing with effort. Gwen's father put an arm out to the wall to catch and steady himself, and knocked against the lamp, which fell over.

It did not break. It fell to the carpet, where it lay on its side, shade askew so that you could see the light-bulb. It was peculiar to see a lamp like that, Gwen remembered thinking.

"Steady now," her father had said, as if he hadn't been the one to almost fall. "Steady as she goes."

It would be tempting to believe that the evening had gotten progressively worse from that point, but in fact, after the lamp was put to rights and they'd all recovered, nobody said anything about Gwen and Avery's father coming in drunk at Avery's slumber party. Sally was packed off to bed, and Gwen's mother and father had said goodnight and gone back into their bedroom not much later, with a blustered warning from Pop: "And don't make too much god-damn noise out here, you little preteen monsters!" The girls laughed and talked and did each other's hair, and they didn't exclude Gwen from their conversation, which Gwen had felt at the time was really different from what her own friends would probably do when she had *her* first slumber party. Kimmy and Casey wouldn't want to have Sally or Avery around; they were like that. Avery's friends were nice. Avery was nice too, letting Gwen stay up with them. The party became fun again, almost hilariously fun—the close call with the lamp put them all in high spirits. It wasn't until later that things got weird.

The lights were out, and they were sitting in the blue glow of the unwatched, muted television, doing a friendship test on each other called Red Roses, Green Grasses, Purple Violets. Red Roses was a series of light pinches down the inner arm, administered by the girl who wanted to test the nature of her friendship with you. Green Grasses was a long sweep back and forth with the fingertips, and Purple Violets was a pair of light taps on the inner wrist. Your friend did it five times on your arm, chanting "Red roses green grasses purple violets . . . Red roses green grasses purple violets," and when she stopped and looked at your arm, you were supposed to be able to see a red, green, or purple tinge to the skin: red meant "friendship," green meant "envy," and purple meant "hate."

16

Beth said suddenly, "Avery, I think your parents are fighting."

"Oh, they always fight," Avery said with a laugh. Gwen looked at her sister in the dark. Avery's eyes and mouth gleamed. She looked pretty. But she also looked weirdly determined.

"They do not," Gwen said.

"Uh, *yeah*, they *do*," Avery retorted. "And you totally *know* it."

At the time Gwen was ashamed that Avery would be so sarcastic about their parents in front of her friends. She hadn't realized how angry Avery was about their father. In the brief silence that followed Avery's remark, they all heard it, from the back of the house: her father's voice, indistinct but loud. Their house wasn't large—almost every word was audible.

I can do whatever the hell I want. This is my house, this is my roof, and I don't have to apologize for shit.

Then their mother's voice, lower, murmuring, less clear.

Then: *"Avery!"*

Avery shot to her feet. Gwen scrambled up too, almost on instinct.

"What?"

"Come back here! I want to talk to you for a second."

His voice was loud. His words were ragged around the edges. Gwen and Avery had heard him drunk many times before—it didn't scare them to hear him this way, not exactly. But Avery's friends were another story. Gwen wasn't scared of her father, but she was scared of what might happen.

Avery looked at her friends. She rolled her eyes. "I'll be right back." She stepped out of the nest of blankets and started down the hallway. Gwen followed.

"What are you doing? Go back out there!"

"No, I want to come."

"Don't—" Avery turned then and glared at Gwen in the hallway, giving her a little push. "Don't wreck it any more than it's already been wrecked," she whispered ferociously. Gwen rarely saw Avery so angry—it was usually Gwen herself who pushed, fought, was mean. "Go back out there and act normal."

Gwen didn't move. She stood still in the middle of the hallway, feeling the carpet cool on her bare feet. Avery finally huffed, turned, and went to the glowing yellow outline of their parents' bedroom door. She closed the door behind her. Gwen inched down the hallway and stood outside.

"Your father wants to apologize," Ma's voice said evenly.

There was a silence. Gwen heard a low noise, like a cross between a sniff and a sob.

"Jesus. Don't cry, kid."

"You ruined my party." Avery was definitely crying.

But Gwen could tell she was trying to keep her voice quiet.

"Don't cry, honey. Come here and sit by Mommy." Some rustling.

"Ah, Christ."

"See what you did, now? See how upset she is?"

"I didn't do anything wrong. Christ. I have a couple of drinks and suddenly I'm persona non grata around here." Gwen didn't know what "persona non grata" meant, but she could tell her father's voice had a sarcastic edge to it. That meant two things: he was still pretty drunk, and Avery was being a crybaby. In the hallway, Gwen leaned against the wall and sighed.

"Why do you always have to have a couple of drinks?" Avery cried suddenly. Gwen rolled her eyes. Avery. Such an actress. "Why couldn't you stay sober for my birthday party?"

There was a moment's silence; then her father laughed—in surprise, almost.

"Don't laugh at your daughter, Paulie."

"She's acting like she's in a goddamn soap opera. Avery. I'm sorry I got a little drunk. But I don't see how it makes any goddamn difference since I wasn't even home all night. And now I'm sitting back here," he went on, "keeping my goddamn mouth shut, leaving you and your preteen queen friends to do whatever you want. So quit your crying and go have your party."

"And he's sorry."

"And I'm sorry. All right?"

"No, it's not all right." Avery's voice was stony.

"Oh, for God's sake. Get out of here. Go play with your friends."

"Paulie."

"I'm *sorry*. Okay? Now get out of here."

There was a furious rustling, followed by soft, fast footfalls on the carpet. Gwen had barely enough time to skitter into the bathroom before Avery burst out into the hallway.

After that, Gwen had known better than to ask her mother if she could have a slumber party. Maybe her mother would have said yes, maybe she wouldn't have. But that was exactly what made this crummy roller skating party even worse: Gwen had just wanted to avoid more trouble, more weird scenes. And all she got was this: hot, moist skates. Orange Tang—not even pop. Grainy cake, with icing that tasted like sugar mixed with Crisco. Laura Branigan, over and over and over—Gwen liked "Gloria," but the DJ had played it three times already. And Kimmy—bigmouth Kimmy—trying to buy her mother something from the food pit.

Gwen looked at the clock as she skated back from the girls' room with Dawn. Only an hour left until six, when the roller rink closed. She felt tired, tired and bored. She was ready to go home and open her presents from her family. Avery, Sally, and her father were supposed to be making Gwen an "ugly cake" this afternoon. Ugly cake was a tradition in their house: deliberately lopsided layers, weird icing patterns, sideways candles. Once, even a half-eaten apple plunked on top—that had made them all laugh like it was the funniest thing they'd ever seen.

"Look at this great cake!" Kimmy said enthusiastically as Gwen and Dawn approached. Gwen gave her an exasperated look.

"It's super, yeah," she intoned, in her most sarcastic voice.

Then she caught her mother looking at her. Her mother's face was curious—and sad, and hopeful. Gwen blinked. Her irritation drained out of her and was replaced by something else—she didn't know what; maybe protectiveness? Maybe. But even that wasn't quite it. Maybe this was what her mother had felt like when she was trying to figure out how to swing a birthday party for her, even if it was just a little stupid one. Gwen leaned against her mother's side, and they put their arms around each other—her mother's arm around Gwen's shoulders, Gwen's arm around her mother's waist. Gwen's mother was skinny like her. It always made Gwen feel better to stand side by side with her mother. Gwen put her ear to her mother's ribs. "Thank you, Mommy."

"Don't mention it," she said.

BAKE SALE
A RUBY OLIVER STORY
E. Lockhart

I don't really like baking.

I like eating stuff that other people bake.

True: Cricket, Nora, Kim, and I used to go over to Cricket's every week and make batches of chocolate chip cookies. But to be honest, I was really more of a tray-greaser and batter-taster than an actual baker. Nora did most of the baking. The one time I took charge of a batch of cookies, something went wrong and the batter was really gloopy; the cookies turned black around the edges, and I got a large burn mark across the center of my palm because I forgot to use a pot holder.

But.

Every year around the holidays, there is this charity bake sale at Tate Prep[1] that raises money to buy holiday gifts for the kids at a shelter in downtown Seattle. It's always a big thing, the bake sale; people get really show-offy. The stay-at-home mothers go all out, and then the non-stay-at-home mothers feel they have something to prove, and go even further out. So it's hardly a matter of a few loaves of banana bread and

[1] The school I go to. It's full of the children of doctors and lawyers and people with big fancy houses on the water. I go there on scholarship.

some sad-looking oatmeal squares. I'm talking about pinwheel cookies with three different colors of batter, cupcakes made to look like ladybugs, cookies decorated like tiny fire engines, and six-layer ultimate fudge.

Quite a number of Tate girls have inherited their mothers' urge to display their talents as domestic goddesses—and if you're the kind of person who believes that the way to a guy's heart is through his stomach, then the Tate Prep Charity Holiday Bake Sale (CHuBS) is a good time to snag a guy. The thing goes on for a week in the entrance hall of the main building, and boys are always waiting on the front steps, trying to get freebies off the girls who are on their way to deliver their stuff to bake sale central.

Not being the domestic goddess type, I stayed out of the whole thing freshman year. Cricket, Kim, Nora, and I did our part only by purchasing and consuming large quantities of baked goods instead of eating lunch. But sophomore year, I had this boyfriend called Jackson: a tall, gravelly-voiced junior who stuck notes in my mail cubby, drank a lot of root beer, and drove an old Dodge that used to belong to his uncle. He and I had started going out in the early fall—and I had never been so happy.

At least, I thought I had never been so happy. Here's what I mean: writing this now, I know that our whole relationship thing was headed for a major breakup debacle that would completely ruin my life[2]—but at the time, I felt we had something close to love.

So. Everyone at Tate Prep has to do a certain amount of community service each term—and what with going to Jackson's cross-country meets, hanging out on weekends, and doing stuff with him after school, I had gotten seriously behind.

That's where the bake sale comes in.

A popular senior girl named April announced it during assembly in early December. I was sitting in the auditorium with Jackson's arm around me, surrounded by his friends. April said the organizing committee needed a few more people, and to talk to her afterwards if interested, and that sign-up sheets for baked goods would go up that week in the Refectory and the main building, blah blah blah.

"Roo," Jackson had whispered as she was talking, his breath warm against my ear, "are you gonna bake me some brownies?"

"What?" I laughed.

"Brownies," he whispered, nibbling on my earlobe. "I love brownies. Like the kind with lots of walnuts. Or those cupcakes with the cream cheese—what are they called?"

"Black bottom."

"Sounds dirty," he laughed, and kissed my neck.

---

[2] You can find out what happened in a book called *The Boyfriend List*. But be warned: it's full of hideous painful details that are not for the faint of heart.

Things between us at this point were already getting a little weird, though I didn't admit it to myself then. For example: I'd seen this note in his back pocket in another girl's handwriting; he'd gone on this completely anxiety-inducing tennis/coffee date with his ex-girlfriend Heidi, and told me he thought she was superbeautiful; we had a fight one time when he said he'd call and didn't; and he'd stopped leaving little presents in my school mail cubby every Monday.

This underlying weirdness made me feel kind of spazzed out, but at the same time, we were having three-hour kissing sessions, and Jackson was saying things like "I never felt this way before."

Anyway. All you really need to know is that when Jackson got me all hot and bothered in the auditorium, breathing in my ear and kissing my neck and asking me to bake things for him, a tiny part of my brain thought: He'll love me more if I make those black bottom cupcakes.

I am an idiot, I know. But that is what I thought.

I ran right up to April after the assembly and offered my services. Partly because of my sorely lacking community service hours. But really because of sex.

"Roo, you're out of your mind," said Nora when I told my friends at lunch. "You can't even read a recipe or remember to use a pot holder."

"So?"

"So, this is hard-core baking," she said. "You could do yourself some bodily harm."

"Oh, please. Do you think Jackson would like the black bottoms or the brownies better?"

"You could just give him a hand job and save yourself a lot of time and trouble," put in Cricket.

"What?" I started laughing.

"I mean," she said, "the way to a guy's heart. It isn't through the stomach—"

Kim leaned across, picked a raisin out of my salad, and jerked her head in Cricket's direction. "Her mind is in the gutter."

"—it's through the nether regions!" Cricket laughed.

"I'm not nether-regioning Jackson," I said. "That's way too advanced."

"Everyone knows it," continued Cricket, ignoring me. "There's a line directly from the you-know-what to the heart."

"Oh, like you're nether-regioning anybody," said Nora.

"I didn't say I was, but I'm not puttering around in an apron, either," said Cricket, smirking. "And I would fully nether-region before I started opening cookbooks."

"Don't bake," said Nora to me, seriously. "I just know it'll be a disaster."

"Don't nether-region, either," said Kim, sweetly. "If you don't feel like it. Just be yourself. He's already your boyfriend."

"I need the community service hours, anyway," I said.

"Well, if you must, you must," sighed Nora. "But put a sign on the stuff you make. So we'll know not to eat it."

I threw a raisin at her.

But I didn't change my mind.

At the first CHuBS meeting, I could see I was way out of my league. April ran the thing with Debra (another highly visible senior girl), and they were talking about silver dragées and meringue frosting and the bakers' specialty shop in Ballard. "We can charge more and raise more money if the things are super-special," said April. She told us that last year the sale had raised $1232, and that this year they were looking to hit $1500. "You can always figure on banana bread and chocolate chip cookies coming in from random people," she went on, "and I know we can count on Bick, Steve, and the Whipper[3] to get their moms to do something spectacular. Does anyone here remember those Santa cupcakes Mrs. Buchannon made last year?" She giggled. "They sold out in an hour."

Debra piped up to say she'd kept a record of what had sold for the most money last year, and though it wasn't scientific because, like, there were forty Santa cupcakes but only twenty-eight snowman cookies,

[3] The Whipper: April's then boyfriend, Sky Whipple, Big Meathead on Campus.

the official declaration was that the cuter it was, the more it would sell.

"So it's up to you, ladies," said April, taking back control of the meeting, "to heat up those ovens and bake cute!"

She started assigning people to specific cute-baking projects: Debra would do snowman cookies, gingerbread men, and something called puffballs; Molly would do checkerboard cookies in red and green, blah blah blah. I was just about to raise my hand and ask if maybe there was actual *organizing* I could do—like calling people to remind them when to bring stuff, or buying white paper doilies or something, instead of this hard-core level of baking—when Heidi walked into the room, flipping her hair over her shoulder.

Heidi, Jackson's ex-girlfriend. The one he said was "superbeautiful." Who he went on the tennis/coffee date with. Who called him up one time when I was over at his house. Heidi, who before Jackson had been one of my sort-of friends, but ever since the tennis/coffee date, not really. It wasn't exactly her fault. I just felt like I had radar and could detect her from forty feet away, including how good her hair looked, how tight her jeans were, how close she was to Jackson, and whether he was

    (1) talking to her

    (2) standing too close to her

    (3) flirting with her

    (4) ignoring her in a tense way.

"Sorry I'm late," she said to April, sliding into a chair.

"No problem. Heidi, I think you and—what's your name again?" April asked, looking at me.

"Ruby."

"Ruby. Heidi, you and Ruby are, like, the junior members, because everyone else was on CHuBS last year. So I'm going to put you two together in charge of cupcakes. They always sell well, and they're not that hard. Okay?"

"Okay," said Heidi.

"Two dozen cupcakes, every day for five days. And Debra's got this great magazine article on decorating she can give you. It's really cute and has all kinds of tips for making them festive. Is that cool?"

A week later, I was in Heidi Sussman's kitchen with my hands covered in batter, out nearly sixty dollars for five days of ingredients,[4] and feeling sick with jealousy at

(1) her enormous house[5]

(2) her three beautiful Irish setters (Jackson loved dogs)

(3) her perfectly round tennis butt

(4) her adorable freckles

---

[4] My dad coughed it up when I told him it was for charity.

[5] Funny, though: I never felt jealous of Cricket's house, which could eat my house for an hors d'oeuvre. Or of Kim's, which has a pool. Just Heidi's, because it was chic and modern and somehow effortless—and because Jackson had kissed her in it.

(5) her tiny, perky boobs[6]

(6) her very differentness from me. Difference. Differentiation. Whatever. How she's kind of sleek and wholesome and future doctor of America, while I'm more thrift shop/fishnet stocking/eyeglass girl.

I knew that it made no sense for me to be jealous. I was the one going out with Jackson, wasn't I? While she was the one carrying a torch.

Really: my butt was perfectly nice, and Jackson himself seemed to enjoy my boobs quite a lot. I didn't actually *want* to live in such a cool, clean house, or get slobbered on constantly by three brainless balls of orange fur. But there I was, the first evening we worked together, feeling like Heidi was a goddess and I was a tree sloth.

Sunday night, we made chocolate cupcakes with chopped candy canes sprinkled on white frosting.

"I need to do remedial decorating to start," I said, so I just tossed the chopped candy in random patterns while Heidi used a tiny cookie cutter to make peppermint hearts on the cupcakes.

She was wearing an apron. I wasn't. She didn't offer me one. I ended up with cake mix on my clothes, frosting in my hair, and a swollen tongue from sucking on so many candy canes.

---

[6] Mine are size medium and require a bra because they are already completely destined for sagginess, but Heidi's just stand up on their own like little chocolate kisses.

I wanted to ask her: Did Jackson say to you that he "never felt this way before"? Does he ever call you, now? What were you talking about with him at Kyle's party, two weeks ago, when the two of you were squashed together on the couch? And when you were going out, did you get around to the nether regions?

When I wasn't having these paranoid and unmentionable thoughts, I was having a perverse urge to mention my boyfriend—pretty much whenever Heidi said anything about anything—and this put me in a state of constant self-censorship. Like, she asked me what sport I was doing spring term, and I almost said, "I'm doing lacrosse again, and Jackson's rowing crew. He's hoping to sit seventh, because the Whipper has eighth pretty much locked." Or when she showed me how to use the Cuisinart to chop up candy canes, I wanted to tell her how Jackson once used his father's coffee grinder to make pimento cream cheese.

But I didn't. I just said "lacrosse" and "cool, they chop up so fast!" So the conversation was pretty strained.

Monday after school was a little better. We made miniature vanilla cupcakes with "ho ho ho" written on them in red icing. Heidi's friend Katarina came over and gave us an in-depth, eighth-hand report on the breakup of April and the Whipper, involving some very slimy behavior on his part and great public dismay on hers[7]—which the bitchy part of me found extremely satisfying, since I was cursing April and her stupid cute baking requirements every minute that I spent at Heidi's. But the nice part of me felt sorry.

"April can give one of these to the Whipper," I said, holding out a "ho ho ho" cupcake.

Heidi laughed. "But can you call a *guy* a ho?" she wondered. "I think it's just for girls."

"Act like one, get called one," I said.

"I don't think you can," said Heidi. "It doesn't sound right."

"The Whipper's not a ho, anyway," said Katarina. "He just had to do something drastic to get away from April."

"You think?" asked Heidi.

"She was trying to control everything he did," said Katarina.

"We should make 'slut slut slut' cupcakes," I joked. "Then there'd be no confusion."

Heidi giggled. "I know some people we could give those to," she said. "But it's probably too mean."

"I don't think a guy can be a slut, either, Roo," said Katarina. "Besides, we can't put all the blame on the Whipper. That Nikki has scammed with three upper-classmen before him."

---

[7] At her mother's annual holiday party, April caught the Whipper in the broom closet not only kissing but *squeezing the boobs* of some freshman girl named Nikki whose mom worked in the same law firm as April's dad.

"Okay, not 'slut slut slut,'" I conceded. "But what about Breakup Cupcakes? We could make a big sign saying Break Up Sweetly, or Leave 'Em with at Least a Cupcake. And we could write on them 'no no no,' 'go go go,' 'slow slow slow,' 'blow blow blow'—and even keep the 'ho ho ho.'"

"I betcha they'd sell," said Heidi, sounding tempted.

"We could charge more for them, too," I added.

"You better not, Heidi," said Katarina. "April will kill you, and you'll never run CHuBS when you're a senior."

And so we didn't.

Tuesday, we made red velvet cupcakes (cocoa and red food coloring), decorated with red cinnamon candies and chocolate icing we made from scratch. Heidi talked about how much she loved to bake, and I nodded my head and wondered if she'd ever baked for Jackson.

"Jackson will like these cinnamon ones," Heidi said, carefully pushing candies into the chocolate edge of a cupcake. "He likes red hots and FireBalls, things like that."

Ag. I couldn't believe she'd brought up Jackson. After two and a half days of successfully avoiding the topic, we actually had a chance of making it through the whole CHuBS experience without ever mentioning him.

Maybe she was just trying to break the tension and talk about the big thing that was looming between us and making everything all weird. Maybe she was trying to be nice and talk like things were normal. But at the same time, it was like she was telling me, "Hey, I know your boyfriend really well. Really, *really* well. I might even know things about him that *you* don't know yourself. So don't think you've got him all locked up. He could want me back."

And maybe she did know things.

And maybe he did want her back, sometimes.

There was no way for me to be sure.

"He's off of those now," I said, although it wasn't true. "He's into watermelon stuff. Like those jelly beans with pink inside, or the Jolly Ranchers."[8]

Wednesday, the cinnamon-chocolate cupcakes didn't sell so well. April was in a pissy mood because of her breakup, and told me and Heidi we had to do better. "I don't know how you think we're going to pass the fifteen-hundred dollar mark if you're just doing the same old, same old," she said, wearily. "Didn't I tell you cupcakes should be big sellers?"

Heidi and I worked the late-afternoon shift at the CHuBS table and ate two of our own cupcakes each, to make it look like we'd done better.

"I would completely buy these," I said. "I don't know what her problem is."

---

[8] What I really meant was, You think you know my boyfriend better than me? Ha. The stuff you know is *so* over. You don't know him at all, anymore. And you probably never did.

"Her problem," said Heidi, "is that her boyfriend ran off with another girl. Come on, Roo, we can cut her some slack."[9]

"Ooh, I know what we should do tonight," I said, changing the subject and trying to pretend like I'd just thought of it, even though I'd been planning it all along. "Let's do black bottom cupcakes."

"I don't know." Heidi wrinkled her nose. "That's not what April wants us to make. They're so uncute. I don't want her to yell at me again."

"Cuteness is overrated," I said. "If you ask me, this entire bake sale has been thus far sadly—nay, disastrously—lacking in true deliciousness."

"What?"

"Everything's just colored sugar and sprinkles and silly Christmas shapes," I improvised. "I think at this point the Tate community is really looking for some hard-core chocolaty cheesecake-y yumminess. As a culture, we've gone beyond the juvenile attraction to snowman cookies. We're ready, collectively, for the black bottom. And if they sell," I added, "April will be happy. You know she will."[10]

---

[9] At that point, I had no idea *what* it would feel like for my boyfriend to run off with another girl. But Heidi did—because Jackson had dumped her only a week before he started going out with me.

And I would find out how it felt for myself, plenty soon enough.

[10] What I was really thinking was: Jackson will know I baked these for him. It's a romantic gesture. He'll be surprised and touched that I remembered what he wished for—and then when he takes a bite, they'll be so good he'll think I'm wonderful by extension. (I am an idiot, I know. I know. I know.)

"Whatever," she said. "If you really want to do it, fine. Have you got a recipe?"

I didn't, but I skipped out of Drama Elective and found one on the Web. Once at Heidi's, the cupcakes were the hardest thing we had made yet: we couldn't rely on a mix, like we had before. We had to work from scratch, using stuff like buttermilk and Dutch processed cocoa. We had to put a tablespoon-sized plop of cream cheese mush on top of the regular chocolate batter, and we made a worse mess of the kitchen than we had any other day.

They smelled amazing, though, and when they came out of the oven, Heidi was ecstatic. "Oh my God, these are soooo good!" she moaned with her mouth full. "Like, a hundred times better than the ones from yesterday." Then she lay down on her beautiful marble kitchen floor and ate the rest of her cupcake staring at the ceiling. "I just have to lie down and concentrate all my energy on this deliciousness," she said.

I got down next to her, and ate one too. We just lay there and chewed, on the cool tiles splattered with cake batter, until we were full and the Irish setters came in from outside, skidding into the kitchen on wet feet.

Thursday morning, I saved three of the black bottom cupcakes for Jackson, squirreling them away from the CHuBS table and wrapping them in tinfoil before April could notice. Then when I saw him between classes, I hid the package behind my back.

"I made something for you."

"You did?"

"Guess."

"What? No, Roo, I'm late for chemistry."

"Come on, guess."

"A painting?"

"No."

"One of those yarn thingummies you make in camp?"

I laughed. "A god's eye? No."

"Oh, oh—" He pointed at me, like he'd just had a brilliant idea. "A lanyard?"

"Wrong again."

"Can I have it now?"

"Yeah." I gave him the cupcakes.

"Excellent. Thanks, Roo. I'm gonna eat one on the way!" He gave me a kiss on the cheek and went to chemistry.

Later, it seemed like he forgot about them. He didn't mention them again, at least.

All that time and money and being with Heidi, and he didn't even remember that he'd wanted them at all.

Thursday was our last night of baking. "I don't want to spend any more money," I said to Heidi. "Let's just see what we can do with the leftovers."

"All right."

We baked vanilla cupcakes from a couple of boxes of mix left over from the miniatures we'd made on Monday, and whipped up a frosting from butter, vanilla, and powdered sugar that were already in Heidi's kitchen.

"It's gonna look boring," said Heidi. "April's gonna be cranky."

"Let's put food coloring in."

We put in all that was left of the red, but there wasn't enough to make a real pink. So we added a little yellow, and the frosting turned a kind of Caucasian flesh tone. We had little cinnamon candies left over, too—and I put one right in the center of a peachy-colored cupcake.

Then I did another. "They look like boobs," I said.

"Oh my God, they completely do!" Heidi cried, holding them up to her chest. "I could use a set of these, don't you think?"

"April would have an absolute attack if we brought them in," I said.

"Ooh, she would, wouldn't she?"

"She'd just about die."

"I know."

We were silent for a moment. I took an index card and a pen off her kitchen counter and wrote, Breasts: Two for a Dollar.

Heidi cracked up. "People would completely buy them," she giggled. "Let's do it."

So we made four dozen breast cupcakes (double the required amount—we even ran out and got more cake mix), and we brought them into school, along with the sign.

They sold out before first period was over.[11]

People were eating breasts in class, in the Refectory, in the hallways. They were holding them up to their chests, laughing.

Nora ate the candy off hers, and then said she was completely freaked out by it because it looked deformed without the nipple. Cricket gave two anonymously to this guy Pete that she liked, leaving them in his mail cubby. Kim wrote a racy note and gave a pair to her boyfriend, Finn.

"Roo's the idea bunny," Heidi told everyone. "I'm the execution."

Even Jackson bought some, and put the following note in my cubby:

"Roo: each bite of your luscious you-know-whats made me think about being alone with you tonight. Can't wait. I'll pick you up at seven. Jackson."

I read the words over and over.

And at that moment, I thought, It worked.

It was worth it.

<hr>

[11] April was furious—until they started selling. Then she acted like it was her idea all along, and did some really good fast talking when the headmaster swung by in the afternoon to ask about some anatomically correct baked goods he'd been hearing about? April slid the sign into her back pocket as he was walking over, then convinced him that he'd been hearing about a bunch of reindeer-shaped gingerbreads.

All the jealousy I felt toward Heidi, the tedious baking, the burns on my hands (because I *did* forget to use the pot holder), the stupid CHuBS meetings—it had all been worth it.

Because it made him love me, even more.

We went out that night and spent most of the time in the backseat of his Dodge.

Now, months after our horrible breakup and the whole debacle that followed it, I am not so sure. I mean, now that Jackson has left me, and hurt me, and humiliated me, and betrayed me; and now that I'm not in the thick of the moment, feeling his warm breath on my neck or basking in the shine of his wide-open smile—I don't think it worked at all.

It didn't make him love me.

In fact, he hardly even noticed.

Actually, it was Heidi who appreciated the stuff I did. The black bottom deliciousness. The idea for the Breakup Cupcakes. The Two for a Dollar sign. What it meant to subvert April's regime and the cute-baking requirement.

True, Heidi was sleek and popular and she wanted my boyfriend. But she wasn't all bad.

I mean, the girl knew how to appreciate a good cupcake.

And that's more than I can say for Jackson.

DO NOT GUT FISH IN ROOMS
Anneli Rufus

The reason Leo took the night shift that June at McDonald's was to make money to take me places. Up and down the freeway in his Dart. Not that I'm so high maintenance. Really it was Leo who wanted to see revolving rooftop restaurants, a shop that sold movie stars' castoff clothes, a belly-dance club that served tarts stuffed with creamy-soft pigeon meat. He wanted to see foreign movies at the NuArt Theatre in Venice Beach, like that Japanese film in which a woman castrates her lover so that she can always keep the part of him she loves the most. *Kichi-san! Kichi-san!* she shouts throatily, cradling her prize.

Leo wanted to see Surrealist sculpture exhibitions, merengue concerts, a séance. Sixteen-year-old guys feel weird going places alone. Especially when they like to dress up. They need girlfriends. I was the one—in a black-and-white checkered sundress and daisy barrettes. The one he said he loved, with a hoarse intensity that evoked a shovel on rocks. The one on whose knees Leo laid his crop-haired head and wept when he was scared. The one to whom, that June, he gave a pearl ring as a birthday gift, from that shop on the pier where oysters hissed in tanks; a customer picked out the one he wanted, a clerk thrust a knife between the shells, prized a pearl from slippery flesh and mounted it in gold.

The night shift was Leo plus four kids not from our town but from the rich town over the hill, where lazy pepper trees draped streets with names like Dapplegray and Roan in long shadows, and glass houses had stilts. The four of them did not need jobs the same way Leo did. They had money already. They just wanted *more,* their *own,* because the money they *already* had—the soft rolls their parents gave them, which rested like pistols in their jeans pockets and purses—was too dull, too easy, just too *there.*

"I feel dorky just having it," said Jeff, folding his arms sharply, shifting his large square bottom on the seat at the coffee shop where we always went after the night shift.

"I get so *embarrassed.*" Alison cringed, hiding her face behind hands whose big freckles looked like spattered butterscotch.

Lisa unsnapped her wallet, gazing into it with large lavender eyes.

"It's such a *drag.*" Showing her teeth, she snapped the wallet shut and flipped it into her white leather bag.

"I mean," said Kit, "it's *meaningless.*"

Kit fished his roll of cash out of his pants pocket and held it, scowling, at arm's length. Flicking his wrist, he made the bills flutter, then rolled them tight again and jammed them back into his pocket. His narrow hips jutted like wings.

"I mean, man, *ludicrous.*" Kit laughed. Leo swooned.

Leo wanted a lot of things, but now he wanted only to be Kit.

Even scowling, and wearing a McDonald's uniform, Kit shimmered gold and bronze and blinding white and glazey blue. The radiance of beaches. As if so much surfing merged his body with sea, sand, salt, sky.

Leo seethed, his own skin splotched with furious red, the rash that never left his too-round chin and flared across his small, vulnerable ears. His slim calves with their dainty ankles were mocked by plump sausage thighs that loomed above and would not firm up even after years of basketball, still wobbling when he walked. His shoulders hung. Leo had grown too tall too young. At sixteen he still stood like the hunched-over outcast at whom normal-sized kids had thrown ice and orange rinds in grade school, shouting "Jolly Green Giant!" and "Quasimodo!" He still flinched driving past the doctor's office in town where his mother used to take him every two weeks, certain that her son had a tumor on his pituitary gland.

At sixteen Leo was almost accustomed to himself. At six foot five, he was not totally freakish for sixteen. He haunted thrift shops, draping himself in the clothes he bought there: bowling shirts and espadrilles, tuxedo trousers, sequined mariachi hats. This is what he liked to wear, going out with me. He was the guy in an emerald satin smoking jacket and cutoffs, eating with chopsticks; the guy with a girl.

But Kit looked good even in a McDonald's uniform. So good, in the same yellow polyester that pulled tight on Leo's thighs and made his rash flame, that strings of girls hung around all night, ordering diet sodas just to watch Kit grill. Sometimes he drove off after work with one of them, sometimes two, in his black '65 Mustang. Sometimes, if they pouted at having to wait, he ducked out to the parking lot with them during his fifteen-minute break.

Leo did not have sex.

The priest said not to. Leo always sighed, *I can't,* pressing his palm to his zipped trouser fly as to an ache. I did not tease; I did not ask him to. I wanted most of all to be away from home, where my senile grandfather lived in the back bedroom, seeing carnivals that were not there. *See that midget?* my grandfather would say. *His name is Weems. He'll guess your weight!* With Leo, in the car, on the beach, his hand guarding his fly, I was not at home. Good.

I was the only one in the world who knew Leo had never had sex, because I was the one with whom he would have had it but did not. He made me swear never to tell Jeff, Alison, Lisa, or Kit. Especially not Kit. As if I'd tell.

One afternoon Leo took me to the Neptune Motel and bought two hours in a room so that later, on the night shift, he could tell his new friends with an offhand shrug, *We went to a motel.* While we were there he memorized the details of the room so that later, offhandedly, he could say, *Huh, there was a burn hole in the headboard and hairs in the carpet and a sign that said,* Do Not Gut Fish in Rooms, *a Paint-by-Numbers picture of a seahorse.* He did not say, later, that he lay beside me writhing on the tight spread of the still-made bed, hand on fly, dark head flipping back and forth, snorting *I can't!* Or that I got up, sat in the orange corduroy chair across the room, and watched the clock, hot wands of sunlight dancing on the floor.

He did not tell them that, checking in and then checking out, he'd signed the register in Kit's name: *Kavanaugh J. Saunders,* in a pointed scrawl.

Afterward, we went to Denny's, where Leo told a waitress what Kit always told waitresses: *Sheepherder sandwich, please. Two buns and a piece of ewe.* A piece of you! He smirked. She looked at me, mouth sour, hands on her hips. Not at Leo, but at me.

Leo was late picking me up one morning. We were going to the beach. I waited in the front room with Grandfather, who was watching wrestling on TV, smoke from his cigar drifting like veils over Pepe the Pirate and Monster Max. *Monster Max is on the turnbuckle!* Grandfather rocked in his chair. *Goldie,* he said, calling me by someone else's name. *Did you see that geek eat the live chicken last night?*

Leo beeped, finally. On the driveway he bounced in his seat, beaming. Pulling out onto the road, he plinked the steering wheel like playing drums. He was changed, floaty.

"Lisa called," he said.

I straightened in the seat. "*Lisa*? From *work*? Called *you*?"

"Yeah." Plink. At a stoplight, Leo smiled idly at the giant plaster shark bolted atop the bait shop. "She said she needed to talk to someone."

"Uh-huh."

"*Uh*-huh." Leo mimicked me, his voice going high but dull, like a penny striking cement.

"So she just called you," I said, "out of the blue."

"She says I'm sensitive."

"Uh-huh."

"I *am*!"

"Uh-huh."

It turned out Lisa had a problem. She was pretty sure she wasn't pregnant, but there was a chance she might be. Her period wasn't due for another two weeks, so she wouldn't know till then.

"Was it Kit?" I said.

"How did you know? Maybe—or else this other guy . . . she was . . . a lifeguard called Chad."

"And she told *you* because . . . ?"

"Bee-*kuzz*." He mimicked me again. "Bee-*kuzz* she feels extremely close to me, she says. Bee-*kuzz* she

46

says I'm sensitive. Which I am. Bee-*kuzz* if she has to—uh—get rid of it, she wants me with her. In the waiting room."

"You."

"Yeah."

"The priest is not fond of those kinds of waiting rooms. Anyway, why doesn't she bring Alison?"

"She says I understand her better."

"Alison's her best friend. Since third grade."

"Well." Leo shrugged. Plink. "Time's not everything."

He pulled into a parking space. The beach shone like a scythe.

Her period came while she was drinking a Yoo-hoo and watching a *Brady Bunch* rerun. She ran out of the bathroom wiping her hands on her trousers, and called Leo.

He was watching TV too. He always sat next to the phone because, those days, Lisa was calling all the time.

After that first call, two weeks back, she called him every day, sometimes several times a day. Leo was glad to talk. She told him how Chad had grunted, *Baby you're so foxy pleeease.* A silence welled between them on the phone. He could not ask, How many times? With him? With Kit? But Lisa guessed, and said, *Yeah, only once.*

Then she said Pink Floyd was cool. He said so too.

47

Their conversations stretched to hours, dotted with taut silences. Sometimes she broke a silence to sigh, shuddery, *I'm so afraid.*

What if I'm—

She made up new words for it: pregeggers, pregno, negprant.

Don't worry, he said. I know he said it, and the way he did, because she called when I was there. He curled up on the couch, cradling the phone, crossing his bolster thighs. *Don't worry.* Shooting a sharp look across the room at me that said at once, *She called me, I didn't call her* and *This is private, so stop listening.*

Don't worry, he said, scratching his nape.

I know.

I know it is.

I will.

A day later he gave me a present: a tight tank top like one of hers.

Those days he kept mentioning her. After we saw *Jules et Jim,* he said, "Lisa has been to France."

"Of course she has," I said. "She's rich."

Ordering turtle steak in a restaurant, he said, "Lisa thinks I'd like it."

"Sure." I sipped my Coke. "Your little friend."

Watching the sun set, he said, "Lisa says sunsets are so romantic that sometimes they're *too* intense."

"Ah, what a slut."

"Why do you act so mean? Lisa's not mean when she talks about you."

"Lisa talks about *me*?"

"Sure, but not mean."

"Lisa. Talks about. *Me?*"

"She only said—what was it?—that you 'aren't exactly Einstein.'"

"Lisa says I'm dumb?"

"You got a D in algebra." He turned and saw me sitting stiffly in the car. "Hey." He patted my knee. "I love you."

The day she called Leo and breathed, *Guess what? Good news!,* in a fierce whisper like the sound of soda flying from a shaken bottle, he had just come home from shopping at Goodwill. Wearing a tartan wool cape and a Foreign Legion hat, he wept at her good news because Lisa was crying too. They cried together, with relief. *I never was so glad to see a Kotex,* Lisa sobbed. She said it was a miracle how what Chad or Kit had done had brought her closer to Leo than to either of *them.* He told Lisa that what really mattered in life was talking, listening, becoming true friends. *Those guys are scum,* Lisa said. *Guys are scum. Screw them.*

Screw them.

Yeah.

Looking down at his vintage Howdy Doody watch, Leo saw that it was still two hours before the time at which he was planning to pick me up and take me to a Chinese opera. Lisa said, *I never could have gotten through this without you.*

Sure you could've.

No—I might just have killed myself.

But you saved me.

You're sensitive.

Well, bye.

Her voice floated, lightly, like a tassel.

Telling himself what the heck, Leo leaped into his Dart. Telling himself he had two extra hours anyway, and that friends celebrated happy times together, he drove to Sav-on and bought a box of Almond Roca and a friendship card. He drove to Lisa's.

But she wasn't there.

A thought struck Leo as he drove along the street under the pepper trees.

He drove to Kit's.

And found her.

She was in the background when Kit, blinking at the light, opened the door a crack. *Hey Leo dude,* he laughed, *not a good time.* Over Kit's golden shoulder, pukka shells gleaming around the firm brown neck, Leo saw Lisa not quite naked. She still wore a pair of black shorts and a sandal. Her hair hung over her eyes. She didn't push it back.

Kit shut the door.

During the Chinese opera, Leo kept time with the drums and gongs, bobbing his head sharply, circling his foot. The actors vaulted, trailing silk streamers the hot pink and yellow of jelly beans. Afterward, in his car, Leo wanted to have sex. He announced it in a voice like cracking glass. But when it came to it, he sat there fully dressed, still zipped, his hands gripping my shoulders as if giving me a benediction. *Now!,* he cried, but no one moved.

"Look," I said quietly. "You want her."

He shook his head wildly from side to side, his ears like small pink dials. "No," he said in his shovel voice. "I love *you*."

"I don't know. Maybe you do. Maybe you don't. But you want her." By now I was out of the car.

"No!" Wet maps of sweat made his bowling shirt sag.

"Yes," I said.

He sounded submerged. "I love *you*."

"Right." I was backing away from the car. I'd left my opera program inside. It flapped on the seat, pink. It jerked to the floor when Leo jammed the engine into gear.

Leo left streaks, the Dart's exhaust making me cough. He drove around the block once, then down to the turn for Channel Street, then doubled back and drove to Lisa's house. She was there this time. He stayed.

A GENIUS FOR SAUNTERING
Thatcher Heldring

"Got no money and you got no car then you got no woman and there you are." —Young MC

> *I have met with but one or two persons in the course of my life who understood the art of Walking, that is, of taking walks, who had a genius, so to speak, for sauntering.*
>
> *Walk with me.*
> *Love, Greta*

Greta

That's it. Those are the words I wrote for Ben in the copy of *Walden* I was going to give him on his sixteenth birthday. The quote is actually from *Walking* by Thoreau, which as a title may have been more fitting for Ben and me—considering how much walking we did, and how much we did while we were walking—but when I saw the weathered old book in the bookstore and held it in my hands, it immediately reminded me of faded jeans and autumn, two things I'll always associate with Ben. Holding the book felt like holding hands with the last two months of my life and smelled like every memory Ben and I shared. Memories we never would have had if we hadn't been two sophomores without cars or any other way home. When I opened the book, I half expected a leaf to fall out from between the pages. I didn't need to think about it, and I didn't ask for a receipt—not when I'd found a way to give a gift that wasn't only a part of myself but also a part of the person to whom I was giving it. Or so I thought.

The first thing I noticed about Ben when he walked into English class and sat down across from me was his jeans. Picture this. In an Abercrombie world of vintage boot cuts, cargo pants, and flat-front khakis, Ben walks in with a pair of 501 slim fits. Now, usually I don't do this. I really am not the kind of girl who talks about someone's pants like that. But Ben, let me help you. With a smile you could light a room with and eyes that always made me feel as though I'd already said what I was going to say, I think it's fair to say Ben wrecked me at first sight. Although technically it wasn't first sight because we were in the same class all freshman year. But sometimes you can see someone every day and there's nothing and then all of a sudden your heart skips a beat and everything is different.

I realized right away that any guy who couldn't get himself to the mall to buy a decent pair of pants wasn't going to make the first move. I could bat my eyelashes and drop my pencil and shake it in front of his desk until graduation, but if the boy isn't going to pick up on it, sometimes you just have to put the writing on the wall. Not literally, though. The last thing I needed was a written note falling into the wrong hands. No, paper trails were not acceptable. I had to get him alone somewhere soon, which, as it turns out, was not as easy as it sounds. Ben may be a bit fashion challenged, but he is not the brooding loner in the corner with the extra Creed ticket. He was, however, always in the middle of a pack of guys. Never a woman in sight, mind you, but also never alone. From the moment school started until they all went off to soccer. I'm not a stalker, by the way, just observant. Which is how I happened to observe that Ben liked to sit on the bleachers after soccer practice, when the rest of the team had gone their separate ways.

The first time I told my best friend, Lillian, about Ben, we were sitting on the grass by the soccer field after practice, watching the boys run their mile and talking about nothing much. I guess I must have spaced because Lillian called me out.

"See anything you like, Greta?"

Busted. "Why? Am I drooling?"

"Practically. Who's the lucky boy?"

Basically, this was the point of no return. I knew once I spoke Ben's name out loud, my crush would go from a fantasy to something real, something I wouldn't be able to take back. I fingered the flower I'd plucked and spoke directly to the ground. "Ben."

"From English class? Cute, smart . . . quiet, bad jeans but sometimes that can work. Now all you have to do is talk to him."

Ben

As usual, soccer practice ends with five laps around the field—a full mile, but most guys cut corners while Coach isn't looking, so it ends up being a little less. In the beginning I try to stay honest, but after three laps I'm following the crowd, cheating here and there to make the run go faster. It's not like I'm going to need the extra stamina standing on the sidelines. Coach says, "Ben, pay your dues and your chance will come." Whatever. The truth is, I only turned out for soccer because my friends are on the team and it keeps me busy. Plus, the varsity girls practice on the other end of the field, and even though we're three weeks into October, the weather is still warm enough for sports bras. Which is all I see as I make my way down the first leg of each lap. I don't even see faces. Just legs and bras. And then, of course, it isn't enough to see them in sports bras: I have to torture myself by trying to picture them naked. Anything to pass the time.

Some of the guys are running shirtless. I'm not quite there with the shirt thing. As a freshman, it wasn't something I paid too much attention to, but now the difference between me and some of these other guys is like night and day. I know some of them put in serious time at the gym and supplement with that protein crap—or maybe more, I don't know—but my guess is that it's mostly a matter of good genes. Either way, there's nothing I can do about it because I obviously can't control genetics, and I'm not about to start tearing my body apart with free weights just to look good with my shirt off.

We're all pretty much spread out as I round the corner for the last half lap. My mind wanders back to the girls. I wonder how many of the other guys are thinking similar thoughts. I wonder how many of them have to rely totally on their imaginations to picture the girls naked. Probably more of them than I think, but you never know. Ahead of me, Chris Brody slows to say something to one of the girls—Vanessa. She laughs. I pass Chris and try not to look at Vanessa. Not because Chris would go after me for looking at his girlfriend, but because I don't want to think about it. Instead, I try to remember whether I threw a bottle of Gatorade in my bag.

I walk it off behind the bleachers and then head for my bag. No Gatorade. Coach talks to us during the cooldown, but no one listens. I find a spot by myself on the top row and take a few minutes to catch my breath. The rest of the guys are gathering up their gear and heading for the parking lot. I see Chris and Vanessa at his car. It's a piece of shit, but it works for him. When he showed up to school in a beater, it took some of the sting out of having to see him with a car. That didn't last long. Because instead of apologizing for having a crappy car, he completely went the other way and owned it. Suddenly it was cool to have a shitty car. I could never pull that off. But there you are. He's driving home in the coolest piece of shit car known to man, and I'll be walking through the woods with a backpack and nothing to drink.

If it were just Brody, it wouldn't bother me too much. Things are always going to be better for guys like him anyway. That's just life. But now it seems every other guy on the team has wheels. It's making things kind of miserable. The funny thing is, a few weeks ago this was my favorite part of the day. Sitting on the bleachers with my best friend, Cooper, and the other guys from our class. Tossing stones at the trashcan. Warm sun, hot girls, nowhere to go. And then one by one guys get cars, and suddenly they have a million things to do right after practice. It was total bullshit. They just wanted to drive off while there was still an audience. At first I tried to hitch a ride home, but you should hear the excuses these guys come up with. I'm almost out of gas. I want to beat traffic on the bridge. Something's wrong with my alternator. Yeah? Alternate this. Now the guys who don't have cars head straight to the bus stop so nobody sees them without cars, walking home.

Greta

I waved goodbye to Lillian and took the last few steps to the bleachers where Ben sat alone, finally. Almost like he'd been left behind and was waiting for someone to return. He must have been lost in thought because when I spoke—in my recollection, the first words ever uttered between the two of us—he looked startled. "You look thirsty," I said, between sips from my water bottle.

Ben blinked twice and shifted his focus to my eyes from a spot somewhere in the near distance. It was so abrupt I was tempted to see if one of the girls was back there in some yoga position. When he did speak, he did so slowly. "Yeah, well, you know, the mile and everything . . ."

"Yeah, I saw. You know, if you ever get tired of running a mile every day, you can always practice with the girls." Did I just say that out loud? All these weeks building up to this moment, and that's what I come up with?

But Ben let me off easy. "I like your flower. Daisy?"

"My name is Greta," I said, shaking my head. "I'm in your English class."

"No, I mean the flower in your hair. Is it a daisy?"

Every drop of blood in my body ran to my cheeks, then fell to my feet. I nodded yes to Ben's question about the flower and paused to regain my cool. "Where's your team?" I asked, reclaiming some self-control. I put down my bag and took a seat on the bottom bench.

Ben

I can't take my eyes off this girl. I try not to stare as she sits down, takes a hat from her bag, and slips her ponytail through the back, leaving the flower from her hair beside her. This is the same Greta who's been sitting across from me in English for three weeks? She's never said a word to me, and now here she is. Things like this just don't happen to guys like me. "Gone," I say to answer her question. "We used to hang out longer after practice, but now everyone pretty much jumps ship when the whistle blows."

"Why don't you get a ride with someone?"

"Don't ask," I say with an eye roll. "What about you?"

Greta gave a look like she was considering the question and then locked eyes with me. "Listen," she said, with a voice that was all business. "Do you want to walk me home?"

I'll be honest. It does cross my mind to ask where she lives, in case it's out of the way, but I stop myself and just say, "Yes." We collect our bags without a word and head toward the main road like it's something we do every day. And for the first time since the start of the school year, I'm actually thankful I don't have a car.

Greta

Our routine never changed from the day it began. Ben waited for me after practice on the bleachers. He said the time it took me to change out of my cleats gave him a chance to catch his breath. There was one day Chris asked me if I wanted a ride home—in the seat vacated by Vanessa, who had left him for the starting goalie—but by then I was long gone for Ben. The first day he walked me home, I think he wanted to ask where I lived, just in case it was over the hills; but he didn't, which was so sweet I can't even tell you. Not that he had anything to worry about. My house isn't too far out of the way. And of course it was fall, and, really, is there a better time of year to be walking home through the woods with a boy you want to throw in a pile of leaves and have your way with? The thing is, whatever did happen or didn't happen, nobody would ever know because on those walks we were all alone in the world. Which is why I think I trusted Ben so completely so quickly. I was never afraid Ben would try anything or make me feel vulnerable, and when you can place your trust in someone like that, it's a *very* big deal. I suppose that's what drew me to him in the first place. He didn't want anything from me. Okay, I know all boys want *some*thing, but I'm not talking about that. Anyway, I don't know about you, but sometimes there is nothing more irresistible than someone who doesn't want anything from you. Without those walks in the woods, if Ben and I had just driven everywhere, I don't think things could have been what they were.

One day after English, Lillian caught up to me in the hallway. "I hope you got a good look," she said, smiling.

"I don't know what you're talking about," I said.

"I'm talking about you staring across the room at Ben for fifty straight minutes. Like he was a Lava lamp."

"I wasn't staring."

Lillian shrugged. "That's okay, because I think I can see what's happening."

"What do you mean?"

"That you love him."

"Do not."

"Do so. You love him. Have you told him?"

"No, of course not."

"So you do?"

"What?"

"Love him."

"What am I, on trial here?"

"Yes, you are on trial. For public swooning and being in love. And I am the judge. So speak the truth. And I remind you, you are under oath."

"I plead the fifth, Lil. I don't know if I love him. And, no, I don't know if he loves me. We're just having a great time together. We just get each other. That's all I know."

"One more question. Have you?"

"Lil! No. Do you think I wouldn't tell you?"

"I don't know. All those walks home through the woods. I don't know what the two of you do when you're alone."

"We—connect."

Lillian looked unimpressed. "And there isn't a small

part of you that wishes he could offer alternative means of transportation? Just once in a while?"

"I can honestly say there isn't."

Ben

Cooper and I are sitting on the bleachers tossing rocks at the trash can, just like the old days. Man, I missed this. Not that things haven't been good. The last three weeks have been insane. Ever since Greta asked me to walk her home that day, we've been in a world of our own. I swore I'd never be one of those guys who got a girlfriend and then blew off all his buddies—the guys who were there for him before the girl came along and would be there long after she left. But in a way, didn't they blow *me* off? Hadn't I been sitting here on the bleachers every day after practice while they drove off to other more important places? My cleats hit the turf as I lay back on the bleachers, barefoot.

"You miss the bus?" I ask Cooper.

"My dad is supposed to pick me up. Guess he's running late. What about you? Waiting for a ride?"

"Nah, just waiting for Greta. We're walking."

"Walking? What do you mean?"

"I mean, walking. I walk her home and then go to my house. It's pretty much on the way."

Out of the corner of my eye, I see Cooper toss a rock at the trash can. It misses by at least three feet. "Shit. That sucks," he says.

At first I think he's talking about his throw, but then I realize he means that it sucks Greta and I walk home. I sit up and shield my eyes. "Coop, listen. Every day I spend at least an hour alone in the woods with one of the coolest girls who's ever spoken to me. The best you can hope for is that your dad is going to show up in a Volvo and drive you home for chores and homework. So, you tell me. What exactly sucks about walking home?"

Cooper obviously misses the point of my little speech as badly as he missed the trash can. "What do you do with your gear?" he asks.

We're quiet for a few minutes. At the far end of the field, I can hear the girls wrapping up practice. Greta will be over soon. After a moment, Cooper speaks up. "So, you like walking home. Does she?"

Good question. We just started reading Thoreau in English class, and even though Greta isn't about to go live with a family of beavers, I know she gets what the book is about. It sounds kind of corny, but there is something peaceful about having that time in the day to be alone together somewhere quiet. I'd still like to have the option of driving home or to the movies instead of walking all the time, but for now while the weather is good, I wouldn't trade that time for anything. And unless Greta is a world-class liar, I think she sees it the same way. Which is what I tell Cooper.

Cooper nods. "All right then. If it makes you happy. And with all that alone time, I imagine it does."

"Hey, what happens in the woods stays in the woods."

Cooper shakes his head and throws a rock at me, missing by a mile.

There is an old stone footbridge that crosses the main road from the soccer field to the woods where Greta and I walk every day. Just across the footbridge two paths lead through the woods to our neighborhood. One path goes up toward a ridge. The other path drops toward a stream. Some days we follow the lower path along the stream. There is a duck pond about halfway down, with a bench on the far side where the sun still reaches even this time of day in November. We sit on the bench and watch the ducks dive for food. Greta does most of the talking. The latest with Lillian's love life. Her Spanish teacher, who nobody can understand. Who's getting too much playing time in soccer. Who's turning sixteen and getting a license and a car next. Other days we take the upper path and walk along the ridge. Now, we've both lived in this area for years, but neither of us knew about the vacant church until we happened to wander into what might have been a garden. You can drive to the church—there is an access road from the main street I found out later—but from a car, you'd never know about the untended patch of lawn in the back. To get there, we have to pull aside a board in the wooden fence that surrounds most of the garden area. Don't ask me how we thought to look in the first place. I wouldn't call us being there trespassing because, first of all, it doesn't look like it belongs to anyone; and, second of all, it's not like we're back there breaking windows or spray painting.

Today we followed the upper path. Greta leads the way through the trees to the fence. Even though we've done this half a dozen times and never been caught, we still act like we're breaking into the Pentagon. Greta reaches the fence and turns to me, holding a finger to her mouth. We crawl through the fence and step onto the grass behind the church. In the center of the yard is a dry fountain with weeds and wildflowers growing all over. On the other side of the fountain from the church is an area of growth that looks like it could have been a flower garden. I head for the softest patch of grass I can find and lie down, using my bag as a pillow. Greta drops her bag and lies down next to me.

"You know, I could kill you and nobody would ever find you," she says, poking me with a stick.

"I think they'd find me eventually. And then they'd come looking for you."

"By then I'll be sitting on a beach in Cabo earning ten percent."

"Ten percent of what?"

Greta rolls on top of me. "I don't know. It's just something they say," she says, tossing the stick.

When the sun dips behind the trees, the temperature drops quickly, and we know it's time to head home before there are people out looking for both of us. Greta pulls her shirt on and takes a sip from her water bottle. I start to put my shoes on. I think back to my conversation with Cooper. Even though I know he was wrong, I can't stop thinking that Greta might not be as into the walking thing as she says she is. I decide I have to know for sure. So as she stands and looks toward the fence, I ask, "You like walking home, right?"

"Oh my God. Have you been talking to Lillian?"

"No, no. It's just . . ."

Greta walks up and kisses me on the cheek. "You have no idea how much I like walking home with you."

I think I have some idea. "That's what I figured. I was just thinking if I had a car we could . . ."

"We could what? Drive home and sit in my basement watching TV? No thank you." She picks up her bag and turns back to me.

I smile. "Good, because to tell you the truth, even if I had a car or you had a car, I wouldn't want to change a thing."

Greta

In a way I'm actually relieved Ben never came right out and said he loved me, because when it comes to boys and things like that, talk is cheap and I'm not, and I know I would have spent the rest of my life wondering whether he said it because he meant it or because he thought he needed to say it. Besides, it was more fun to look for the truth in the signs that don't lie. The way he touched my hair before he kissed me. The way he always let me choose which path we took home. The way he wasn't afraid to challenge me. We never fought, but we didn't always agree.

We were on the bench by the duck pond one day when I asked Ben if he ever wondered what people thought about us.

"What do you mean?" he asked.

"Like, why we walk home all the time . . . that kind of stuff."

"Cooper asked me about it once."

"What did he ask?"

"Basically he wanted to know whether we liked walking home."

"What did you tell him?"

"That I did. And that you did too."

"That's it?"

"That's it. Why—did I say something wrong?"

"No. I'm just surprised . . ."

When I left the sentence hanging, I knew part of Ben wanted to leave it alone and move on to something else. But he must have sensed it was important to me, so he took the bait.

"Surprised about what?"

"That you're so cool about not knowing whether people are talking about us, and if they are, what they're saying."

"First of all, of course they're talking about us. But there's not much I can do about it. And as for what they're saying, I don't really care. To hell with them."

"How can you not care?"

Ben paused. "I care what I think and what you think. But their opinions don't really matter. At least not about this."

"Okay, if you're so 'whatever' about what other people think, why does it bother you so much that Chris Brody has a car and you don't?"

I don't think Ben was ready for that. We'd never talked about Chris. Or even very much about cars. But like I said, I'm observant, and I saw how he watched Chris drive off every day.

"That's different. That's what he has, not what he thinks."

"Why do you care what he has? I thought you said you didn't even want a car."

Ben rocked his head around in exasperation. "I said even if I had a car, I wouldn't want anything between you and me to change. Big difference."

I stood up and stretched before replying. "I still say you're better off appreciating what you do have instead of spending time worrying about what you don't. Who cares about the rest of them?"

"That's what I just said! Anyway, I'm not sixteen and I don't have a car, so it doesn't matter."

"But you will be soon. And then anything is possible. I just hope you mean what you're saying."

Ben

It's the morning of my sixteenth birthday and we're standing in front of my uncle Carl's garage. With a tug, Carl pulls the garage door open and fumbles around for the light. "She hasn't been driven since Paul went to school, six years ago," Carl tells me, reading my mind. The bulb hanging from the ceiling flickers to life and enough light to see fills the garage. Carl reaches beneath the front bumper and works the canvas free. "You should stop by next week. Paul will be home for Thanksgiving," he says as he moves around the car. He pulls the cover back to reveal a Karmann Ghia— an older model Volkswagen. They don't make Ghias anymore, but this car is definitely one of the finer things VW has ever manufactured. Cherry red exterior, two doors, slope nose with oversized headlights and original fenders. Carl gives me and Dad the tour. He's loaning me the car indefinitely, at no cost, to clear space in the garage for his workshop. He shows us the interior. Black vinyl bucket seats, A/C on the dash but no CD player, of course. Not in a car this old. Not even a tape deck. The Ghia is a three speed but will do just fine on the highway, Carl explains. With four cylinders I won't be winning any road races against some of the guys with newer cars, but it occurs to me I can give Chris Brody and his piece of shit a run for his money.

Speaking of Brody, Vanessa finally dropped him. And even though what's bad for him is fine by me, it also means there is a free seat in his car. Awhile back he asked Greta if she wanted a ride home. She said no, of course, but it freaked me out a bit. Which is part of the reason I know taking this car is the right move, even though I said what I said about not wanting anything to change. What I've realized since then is that things have a way of changing even if you don't want them to, so I can either make them change in a way I like, or have someone like Brody change them in a way I don't.

Dad and I drive the car from Carl's straight to the DMV, where I pass the test and walk away with a license. The car will need at least an oil change and probably a full tune-up, but everything runs well enough to make it the mile or so home. Greta knows nothing about this. As a matter of fact, I didn't either until this morning. Dad just came to the breakfast table and said, "Get your coat. We're going to Carl's." Now, back at home, I call Greta.

"We still on for today?"

"You know it," she says. "I have something for you. I can't wait to give it to you."

"I have something to show you, too."

"What is it?"

"Not now. I'll show you when I get there."

"Are you walking over?" she asks.

Not anymore. "Not exactly. See you soon."

Greta

Not exactly. How can two little words that are meant to say nothing tell you everything? I remember something very deep in my subconscious stirred as soon as they were spoken. Something stronger than butterflies, weaker than dread. *Not exactly.* Not just a monster under the bed, but something real and unexpected. Something not in the plans. *Not exactly.* Ben was supposed to ring the bell, come inside, kiss me, and tell me he couldn't wait to see my gift. To open the book, read the words I'd written to him, and tell me he loved me and that he would walk with me forever. *Not exactly.* So when Ben called again moments later from his cell phone—did he run here?—and told me to come outside, I knew . . . that it was all wrong.

I told him I'd been chopping onions. There was no other way to explain to Ben why there were tears in my eyes when I came outside and saw him standing there with that car. I stood under the streetlight with my breath snatched away, listening to him talk about bucket seats and fenders, nodding like a bobblehead. I tucked the copy of *Walden* inside my coat; Ben never noticed and never asked. When he stopped talking and we were left in silence, I couldn't bring myself to mention it. It never occurred to me that when people get excited, they lose themselves in the moment and forget really important details, like the fact that your girlfriend told you she has a gift for you she can't wait to give you. I told Ben I wasn't feeling well and ran inside.

Ben

There is a grinding sound when I shift the car into gear. Replays of what just happened spin through my mind. Greta hardly said a word. At first I thought she was too excited to speak. It probably didn't help that I got a little carried away showing her the car. She didn't even have a chance to show me her present before she got sick. That was weird. I want to believe it was what Greta's mother said it was, a bug going around—that it would pass the next day—but I can't shake a really sick feeling that something was very wrong. Before long, I'm trembling too bad to shift gears. I don't want to lose Greta. My plan was to show her the car and then drive her to the church. We've never seen it at night. I thought it would be the perfect place for her to give me her gift. I had a feeling it was something important to her—not just a DVD or a pair of jeans—but something only I would understand. Besides, I like my jeans.

The next day I leave a message with Greta's mother. I don't know if Greta never got the message or if she just didn't have a chance to call back, but for whatever reason, she doesn't return the call. I consider going over to her house but don't. It's not the right move. I'll see her tomorrow. We can drive up to the church after practice, and I'll ask her if there was something she wanted to give me. I know whatever the problem is, we can figure it out. It's not like we just became two totally different people overnight. I tell myself this and try to breathe a little easier. And try to imagine the look on Chris's face when he sees the Ghia in his parking spot.

Greta

Ben called. He wanted to know how you were doing and if you would like him to drive you to school.
Mom

That's the message I found on the refrigerator Sunday night, the day after Ben's birthday. At the time, I was getting close to forgiving him for not asking about his gift. After all, it wasn't entirely his fault. But reading the note sent me reeling for a chair. This was about more than just the book. Seeing the message was the moment I found myself hating, I mean *hating* that car. And the more I hated the car, the more I think I loved Ben. Innocent Ben, who had fallen under the spell of this temptress with her bucket seats and over-sized headlights, just as he'd fallen under my spell. God, were boys that easy? He could be won over by a car as effortlessly as he could by a human being? But what really made me go to pieces was realizing for

73

the first time that Ben would be driving to school. And home from school. It was becoming miserably clear that whatever we had was slipping away.

I said before that sometimes you can see someone every day and there's nothing, and then all of a sudden, for no reason, a light goes on. Well, the minute word got out that Ben had this new car, girls who didn't know him from Adam were suddenly speaking his name like he was the second coming of Elvis. Even Lillian, who found me in the locker room before practice. "Greta, there you are. Why aren't you out there enjoying this?"

"*Enjoying* this?"

"*Yes!* Do you know what kind of jealousy shit storm you've created? The car . . . the boy . . . Greta, you've got it all! And Ben has been looking all over for you. Vanessa asked him for a ride at lunch, and do you know what he said?" Lillian took a breath and answered her own question when it was clear I wasn't in the mood. "'Sorry, it's a two-seater!' I swear she's still in the hallway counting on her fingers trying to understand." Lillian leaned her head toward mine and looked me in the eye. "Greta, what's wrong? You're not happy?" I shook my head. Lillian pressed on. "Is it Ben? I thought everything was great."

"It is. It was. It was perfect. That's the problem. Things were perfect. And now it's all different."

"Why? Greta, is it about—the car?"

"You think I'm jealous of a car?"

74

"I didn't say that exactly. But are you?"

"Well, you saw the way everyone is looking at him now, talking about him. Before today I was the only one looking at him. He was mine. I found him. I saw him first."

"Greta, that'll pass. It'll be ancient history by the end of the week. And then nobody but you will be looking at him. Just like before."

"It's not just that."

"What else?"

"Don't you think if he liked things the way they were he would have let things stay the same? Instead of changing everything by getting a car? If he wanted a car all along, then it just means he didn't really enjoy walking home with me. That he just wanted—"

"Greta, stop. You are reading *way* too much into this. Ben got a car for his birthday. He got a little attention at school. So what? Wait till after practice. He'll be there like always and then you guys can talk."

"And then what?"

"And then what, what?"

"And then what do we do? Drive home? That's the whole point, Lillian. I don't know what we are anymore."

Ben

It's after practice and I'm on the bleachers in a pair of warm-up pants and a sweatshirt. Two days have passed since my birthday, and we're well into

November. The warm days of early fall are gone. The weather is going to turn soon and it will be too cold and too wet for walking. For the thousandth time I go over the episode at Greta's in my mind. The sudden illness, the unreturned phone call. I can't figure it out. For the first time since we started going out, we went an entire day without seeing each other. Has she been avoiding me, or is this all in my head?

Across the field, she approaches, bag slung over her shoulder, head down. No wave from a distance. No smile. My heart is racing, but it is from dread, not anticipation like all the days before. I dig deep, searching for something I could have done wrong, hoping it's something I can undo so that we'll be okay again. So that we can get in the car and drive to the church like I'd planned to do the other night. Like any other day, almost. When Greta reaches the bleachers, I can see something in her eyes is different.

"You look sad" is all I can think to say.

"Ben . . ."

"Greta, if I did something, if you're mad at me, you have to tell me. Because I can see something is wrong, but I can't figure out what it is. So you have to tell me because . . . Look—how about this—there's still some light. Let's drive to the church."

"Ben, we can't go there. Not anymore. That was before."

The life goes out of me when I hear her say

"before." It doesn't matter what I've done or what happened. The way Greta said it, wherever we are now, there is no path back to before.

Greta

Let's drive to the church. That's what did it. That's what broke my heart once and for all. That he could even think of driving to the church told me everything I needed to know. I know he didn't mean it that way, but it sounded so cheap. Like driving to some secluded point where people go to make out. Had we really been seeing things so differently this whole time? Had it really been about getting me alone every afternoon, and a little walking was just the price of admission? Well, if it hadn't been before, it would be from now on, at least in my mind. But for the moment, I had to say something to Ben to make him understand. But how do you tell someone you love more than ever that he's betrayed you just by driving to school? So I said the only thing I could manage before turning away.

"Thank you for walking me home."

THE DRIVER: ME AND MARTY BECKERMAN
Ned Vizzini

When I walk down the streets of New York, which I do a lot because I'm a writer and we don't get cars, I never look all that hot. I skitter; I dart; I chomp at the bit; I hold fear behind my eyes; I bend over so I move more quickly, like a jockey. And, yeah: I talk to myself.

"Death."

Everybody's got to have something.

"Death."

It works for me.

"Death."

Nobody notices anyway.

"Death."

I say it when I'm frustrated, which I always am. I say it when I'm stressed, which I always am. I say it when I'm late and when my cell phone is ringing and when I wish it upon everyone else and when I wish it upon myself. I say it when I wish I *was* everyone else. But the sad thing is, I say it when I'm happy, too—to clear my mind, to remind me what I'm up against. My mantra.

"Death."

I get it from my father. He has all the expressions; "death" goes hand in hand with "name of the job, name of the job," which he repeats when he's at loose ends but knows he has to get something done, usually after getting up from a session with the History Channel. Death and work, those are what drive my father, and where death and work intersect, at that fun spot in the Venn diagram of life, we get jealousy.

According to the dictionaries it's different from envy, by the way, and envy is what we're really talking about. *Envy* is the delicious "ill will because of another's advantages, possessions, etc." while *jealousy* is just lover stuff, "resentful suspicion." Sometime back in 1960 they morphed into the same word, though, and dictionaries never caught up: jealousy and envy, right next to each other at the bottom of the well, looking up at the other words, each one jealous and envious of the other.

I picked up jealousy early on and never let go. I found it to be the best motivator, better even than sex, because it started before sex and continued on as sex got left behind. My jealousy never let me down; it just telescoped out, refining itself, grabbing at better and better targets until in 2001 it found the best, a bête noire that keeps me true—a writer named Marty Beckerman, a hero for me to run after until I hit death for real.

But first it was video games. Super Mario when I was nine, blocky but strangely narrative, as good an encapsulation of the human condition as any book I was reading at the time. Sometimes you were big, and sometimes you were small. Sometimes you could kill your enemies, and sometimes they killed you. The only thing you had for sure was yourself, and you had to keep moving forward; there was a princess to save, plus it was always best to have the most coins. Mario *was* life.

Something happened after I played four hours of Mario, though; a little light went on in my child's head and asked: What are you *doing*? It wasn't my mom's voice, telling me that it was time to go outside, and it wasn't my father's voice, telling me that it was his turn to play. It was the Driver, and it presented its case well: You're either a consumer of culture or a producer of culture. Which do you want to be?

Death.

People *made* Mario, see; they put it together from scratch in a way that involved the heart of a computer— the magic. They created it from nothing, and I just used it. What a dork. I couldn't stay in that position.

So I started designing video games.

The people who really did it used computers—I knew that much—and employed things called *programming languages,* which apparently meant the BASIC scripts that I saw in *KIDS! Discover.* But the only tools I had to make video games were graph paper and Dixon Ticonderoga pencils. I began to sketch out desert levels, with palm trees.

"What are you doing?" Mom would ask, poking

into my room. My desk lamp nearly scorched my pet lizard, Xerxes, who always sat on my shoulder.

"Designing a video game, Mom."

"Oh." She would leave. My lab was closed to outsiders early on.

Up next were comic books. I bought them, read them, *grokked* them, and then the Driver rose up in me and asked: Producer or consumer, Ned? Because you can't be both.

So I tried to make comic books: I went over to a friend's house to watch some rented Marvel video that purported to teach you how to draw them in the length of the video, meaning, uh, sixty minutes, and that was where I learned to weep silently. As the hands on the screen drew rippled heroes and my friend drew rippled heroes, I drew what looked like a crash test dummy carved from a potato. I couldn't do it; I was a failure.

Death.

The Driver kept driving, though; at twelve it led me to read everything George Orwell wrote that my grandmother owned, and I became jealous of *him*. His essay "Such, Such Were the Joys"; I was jealous of that. The fact that he wrote it and not me, that made me angry. He was dead and still producing culture, and I was alive and just consuming it. How lame!

There was an advantage to this new medium of hatred, though—I could catch up quickly. I didn't need special tools to write. The only language I had to understand was English. My graph paper and my Dixon Ticonderoga pencils were overkill; I could use plain lined paper and any old pencil or pen. So I would finish an Orwell essay and immediately appease the Driver by cobbling together one of my own.

I didn't show my writing to anyone but my parents, but I had a feeling it was good; I was a chameleon who could write anything. I moved forward. Writing was the gig for me, where I could most easily and cheaply experience art, suck it into my consciousness, get jealous of the fact that I hadn't made it, and spit it back transformed, morphed into something of my own. You can get addicted to a thing like that.

Rapidly, in a way that would make other people jealous, I began imitating the work of confessional essayists in a local alternative newspaper, *New York Press*. Once I got published there, I moved on to a first book and then a second; but the Driver was never happy. I dented it most mortally when I got that first piece in the *Press,* when I first saw my name in print— the world exploded for me, and I walked through high school not just happy for myself, but happy for the sum of flesh around me. But the next day the Driver was curious: What next?

When I was twenty, the Driver found its best lure. *New York Press* printed a cover story written by a (and before long he wouldn't need an "a" in front of his name) Marty Beckerman, from Alaska. Marty was seventeen. He was excellent with ages; although two and a half years younger than me, at every critical juncture—his *Press* cover, the publication of his book *Generation S.L.U.T.*—he always managed to be on the younger side of the two-and-a-half-year gap, to make himself three years younger, in a different class.

Marty was a chewed-up, sucked-in, spat-out, and improved version of *me*—it was terrifying that someone had been on the other side of my equation. He wrote from a nerd perspective like I did; he wrote about the vagaries of girls and the decrepitude of American high schools and colleges, but he did it with a cavalcade of curses and capitalized words and cracked-out, self-referential phrases and "Praise Jesus" refrains and reckless hate that was, well, astonishing. It was thrilling to read.

We got in touch quickly, in one of those find-the-other-person-on-the-Internet-only-you-don't-remember-who-e-mailed-who-first ways. I liked him, just as I liked his writing; he was quick and bone-dry and you couldn't one-up him at bringing yourself down, at least personally. He had a concept for this new book, which he intended to sell. He wanted to come to New York to do so, and we decided to room together at my apartment for the summer.

Marty moved quickly in New York; he conquered it. He came in June, and yeah, we went out and got drunk—but in the house during the day it was all business, him writing his book while I wrote mine. His work ethic was inspiring; he put on punk music of the fastest, catchiest kind in my living room and sat at his laptop (which I helped him buy) and snipped at keys and leaned back, snipped and leaned back, until he said he was going out for lunch. He used plastic cups, bowls, and silverware so as to not waste time on dishes. If he was working, I had to be working, and so I moved through my book afraid to show it to him, closing it when I took my trips to the bathroom (I ate in).

"Wow, I get about twenty-five hits a day on my Web site," I told him one day, resigned, trying to make a joke of it.

"Really, man? I get, like, four hundred," he said.

I gulped. I set to work on the Web site. The Driver did not let up. Now I get two thousand hits a day according to that stupid LiveStats software that probably counts people in the Philippines turning on their computers as hits, but I'm sure Marty gets more, no matter how you measure it.

By the end of the year, Marty had sold his book; I never asked how much he got, but he complained about the advance. A funny thing had happened that summer I spent with my bête noire, though: we'd become friends. We had conversations that were like little books of their own.

Marty: "So, would you rather be the world's greatest novelist or a rock star?"

I paused. "Can't think of any reason not to pick rock star."

"Me too."

Another day: "I used to want to kill myself like Kurt Cobain, but that's so passé. I'd like to die by assassination."

"Marty, writers don't get assassinated."

"But thinkers do, Ned. *Thinkers* do."

Marty was rife with issues like I was rife with issues. He had problems with women like I had problems with women. His Driver was even worse than mine, driven as it was by fame. I was never interested in fame: I understood through a nasty scrape after high school that it killed people; it killed families; it made your life not your own. I was interested in success, in production, in adding to the culture instead of just sucking off it—not in being famous. Fame and writing, I felt, couldn't mix. Even your most famous writer, he's about as famous as Yo-Yo Ma. But Marty seemed destined to destroy that theory.

The next year it got worse. Marty got an assignment from *SPIN* to interview Hunter S. Thompson, and he came to New York City and rode up to Thompson's hotel and hung out with him and his girlfriend (and Marty had *his* girlfriend along, too, whom I had dumped the previous fall—a victory for my side) and did his interview. But Marty was no fool; while he had Thompson in the room, he got him to blurb his book.

Marty Beckerman got a blurb from Hunter S. Thompson. Shit.

Not much I could do about that one. When it came to places in history, to the race against death, a blurb from Hunter S. Thompson meant a lot. I was shattered. I called my dad.

"I'm so jealous. I don't know what to do. I'm a failure."

"Who cares what that old pervert Hunter Thompson has to say?" my dad responded.

I laughed. "Well, lots of people—"

"Did you ever think about something, Ned? Did you ever think about the fact that you're the only one who can control what you do?"

"Well, yeah."

"Why are you wasting time worried about someone else, then?"

"Is that Ned?" my mother yelled from the background. "Tell him jealousy is a sin! God forbids it."

"Seriously, Ned. Where among these feelings of hopelessness do you hide the fact that *you* wrote a book too and that your agent is about to sell it?"

I hadn't thought about that. "It comes in somewhere."

"Right. Thinking about other people is a waste of time. Do your thing."

I hung up the phone feeling better. Not all the

way, but pulled back from the deepest pit, holding on to the wall. A week later my agent did sell my book—for more money than I ever thought I'd see from my writing—and for a few months after that, the money cushion kept the Driver at bay. That's how the world measures success, with money, and if I was getting it I was doing something right, right?

But art isn't judged by money. It's judged by death. By a lack of money. So I'm back at the beginning again: a scrappy kid with everything to prove, trying to produce and not consume.

Marty Beckerman is the hero and I am the also. He is the genius and I am the runt. But he's also a cool guy, and maybe our summer affected him the way it affected me—made him know that this brutal, jealous life of art was the one for him, because the moments of triumph are so pure. Somebody likes your writing, sends you an e-mail: that's a pure thing.

Marty runs ahead of me, younger and better, but ahead of him is something better still: the grown version of me, the version I can become if I stick to this game, keep reaching. That's who I'm really jealous of.

WHY I'M JEALOUS OF NED VIZZINI
Marty Beckerman

Wow! Ned Vizzini has an Enormous _____!

At least, that's what I hear from the ladies. Of course, someday our biographers will ponder whether Ned and I ever shared a secret, passionate homosexual tryst—too shameful to admit, too delicious to resist—so I might as well admit it now: Ned Vizzini has an Enormous _____. At least, that's what I hear from my ex-girlfriend.

"It's monstrous," she once said. "I mean, like, yours is okay—don't get me wrong—but Ned's . . . wow . . ."

But this is a reminiscence of Ned's many good, jealousy-inducing qualities, not the endless sensitivity of that sweet little girl whom Lucifer cursed upon my life. So I'll start with the Question of the Day: Why am I jealous of Ned Vizzini?

Well, there are the obvious reasons: He's tall (5'11") and I'm a fucking Jewish midget (5'5"), so he immediately gains Alpha Male status. He's also scored with more chicks than I have; hangs out with cooler, more famous people; sells more books; gets invited to more parties; and has his own apartment in a trendy Brooklyn neighborhood. Also, Ned Vizzini has an Enormous _____!

But the real reason I'm jealous of Ned, besides the

fact that he has an Enormous _____ , is that nobody dislikes him. In fact, most people who know the guy consider him a great friend and charming lover, which is not quite the Story of My Life. (Actually, for the story of my life, you should pick up *Gender Genocide,* a novel from the 1970s about a planet of Feminist Lesbian Aliens who come to Earth and exterminate All Male Pigs.)

Anyway, I'd estimate that—oh, I don't know—ninety percent of the people I meet take an immediate dislike to my personality and sense of humor, whereas nobody has any complaints about Ned. This is probably because I'm a total asshole and he's a nice guy; but why am I a total asshole and why is he a nice guy? Oh Lord Jesus, why did you make Ned Vizzini a better person? Oh Lord Christ, why did you give Ned Vizzini an Enormous _____?

Indeed, this divergence of social aptitude is apparent whenever Ned and I walk into a party together: I'll usually sit on a couch by myself, paralyzed by agoraphobia and misanthropy (it's an interesting mix of Fear and Hatred for People), while Ned proceeds to control the entire crowd—even if he's never met anyone in attendance—with his gregarious, self-effacing jokes and devilish good looks (and Enormous _____). And every time, I'm the bashful little guy who doesn't talk to anybody; sometimes a Kindhearted Girl will approach the couch, trying to engage me in conversation.

"Hey there," this Girl will say. "What's up? Are you having a good time?"

"Go die, you fucking bitch," I cry into my glass of Southern Comfort. "Lucifer's little puppets, that's all you bitches are, every last one of you."

What the fuck is wrong with me? Why do I live my life like a TV comedy in which I'm both the studio audience and the main performer? Why do I say these things that entertain nobody but me, alienating everyone who might otherwise consider being my friend and/or lover? Is my instant gratification really worth the long-term misery and loneliness I'm causing myself?

Questions, Questions! Questions that I've ignored for Too Long! And who could blame me? Who wants to look in the mirror every morning and see a despicable, worthless shrew of a human being stare back? Who wants to admit to the Wretched, Irredeemable Nature of His or Her Own Existence?

But Ned! Oh Lord, Ned is different. Ned is the extraordinary kind of person who takes *joy* in other people's accomplishments. Ned wants others to *succeed*. Ned wants the World to be a Good Place for everyone, not simply himself. And this makes him beloved by friends, welcomed by strangers, and endlessly attractive to nubile strumpets.

In La Casa de Ned, everyone is a Winner. In the House of Beckerman, all others are worthless, aimless sycophants upon the festering corpse of Human

Existence. And even Human Existence is questionable under moral scrutiny: The World is a Horrible Place, filled with Horrible People doing Horrible Things to one another. No way in hell do I want most other people to succeed; I want most other people to Kill Themselves.

Incidentally, all the girls I've ever loved in my life invariably think I'm pathetic, narcissistic, clingy, insecure, bitchy, codependent, insensitive, and a mistake to have ever loved/dated/met. And they're probably all correct in these assessments. There is no good reason for my continued existence, but I'm too fucking in love with myself to commit suicide.

Narcissistic? Shit, it's not *my* fault that I'm the greatest writer of my generation, is it? It's not *my* fault that I'm capable of literary feats that even Shakespeare would've salivated over, don't you understand? It's not *my* fault that I'm the only interesting person left in the World, wouldn't you agree? It's not *my* fault that when the Universe finally contracts upon itself and all life is reduced to Nothingness, the only two names that shall live on for All Eternity are that of Almighty God—the Creator Himself—and Martin Beckerman. It's not my *fault*, you simpletons! Why can't any of you *process* that information?

Oh . . . Ned . . . right . . . this is all supposed to be about *Ned* . . . Ha! Ha! All about *Ned,* it's always all about *Ned.* Well, *Ned,* that's coming to an End, *Ned.*

Because the letters of Ned rearranged spell End, just like it's the *End* for *Ned*. That's right, Ned. Just because people *like* you doesn't mean that you're *better*, does it, *Ned*? Just like you're always better at *everything*. Aren't you, *Ned*? Aren't you *better* at *everything*? Fuck! Fuck! Shit! Fuck! _____! Shit! Fucking Piss! Balls!

And that's why I'm proud to say that Ned Vizzini is the best friend I've made since high school—my best friend with the Enormous _____. And I know, because I've been sucking it for a thousand words.

SHE'S MINE
Jaclyn Moriarty

I just want a boy to hook his pinkies in my ears.

I'm not sure why.

"My Eustachian tube is not a guitar string," I pointed out to Kara. "Leave it alone."

"Not until you leave my cochlea alone," Kara shot back, very cold.

She didn't even have to check the ear diagram. She just remembered the word.

We both looked up and found the cochlea, just above the Eustachian tube.

It was shaped like a snail.

"DON'T YOU EAT MY COCHLEA!" Kara yelled, before I got the chance, and then we nearly fell off our chairs.

"Okay now," said Mr. Bayley, but he said it in a happy way. I think maybe he was proud that his ear diagram had made us laugh.

What I really wanted, though, was a boy to hook his pinkies in my ears.

I thought about that on the way to assembly, which is after biology on Tuesdays.

I didn't care when it happened. It could be at assembly, right now.

Only I had to be leaning back, lost in thought, and

the boy had to approach from behind, stealthily, and place his little fingers in the upper part of my ears. (I mean the part that curls inward like the edge of a Frisbee.)

And he had to tug on my ears as if to suggest, humorously, that he could lift me up and into the air, with nothing but his pinkies in my ears.

Another thing: the boy had to be Nero Belmonte.

At assembly, the chief librarian told the school about some amazing innovations in her borrowing procedures. A group of thin students played their flutes for us. The principal followed up with some amusing small talk, which I did not quite catch, as Kara was crunching on corn chips.

I didn't want any corn chips because I wasn't hungry.

I was angry.

Here's why: Nero Belmonte was way across the auditorium, leaning against the window ledge, making no effort whatsoever to put his fingers in my ears.

And I didn't think he ever would.

Unlikely things do happen, see, but not if you imagine them first. If you imagine them, you make them so unlikely they evaporate. And it was clear to me that this was Mr. Bayley's fault: if he hadn't taught us The Ear that day, I wouldn't have gotten the idea about Nero's little fingers, and if I hadn't gotten the idea, well, maybe it would have happened on its own.

I fixed my gaze on Mr. Bayley. He was sitting up on the stage with the other teachers, his cleats stretched before him and his soccer ball resting on his lap. He's the soccer coach at lunch times. He noticed me staring and waved, then shrugged to show that he, like me, found school assemblies boring and stupid. I gave him a mean sneer. That startled him.

Then I felt guilty, so I started pulling strange faces, as if the sneer was just a part of my repertoire, and he seemed relieved and laughed. He even tried a half-hearted clown face of his own, and tossed the soccer ball into the air.

At that exact moment, the principal finished his small talk, held the microphone close to his teeth, and announced: *"Impromptu Time!"*

So everyone stopped breathing.

It's your first instinct when Mr. Kershaw announces Impromptu Time: stop breathing. Then you remember how difficult it is to hold your breath long enough to die.

So you start breathing again, and you try one of the following techniques: (1) lower your gaze so as to stare at: your fingernails, your knees, or the knees of the person next to you; (2) lean over and untie your shoelaces, or the shoelaces of the person next to you; (3) drop to the floor and crawl underneath your chair.

You can also stare Kershaw right in the eye, if you're brave enough to try a double bluff. Or you can get up and run out of the room, if you're stupid enough to believe no one is going to stick their sneaker out and trip you.

If you have a friend like Kara, you use this technique: lean toward one another and make a curtain of your hair.

So Kara and I were trying to unbraid Kara's hair at high speed (her fingers were cheesy from corn chips), and giggling in a quiet, snorting way because we couldn't believe Kara had braided her hair on a Tuesday. Mr. Kershaw was pacing the aisles.

He was tossing his microphone from hand to hand like someone on *American Idol*. He passed us by with a *"hmm,"* wandered into the younger grades, and stopped a few rows back.

He had someone.

We both straightened up and breathed out, and Kara started rebraiding her hair.

Behind us, Mr. Kershaw said, "You're the lucky lady, and what's your name?" and I got the strangest sensation. There was a gasping sound in the microphone, and then I knew for sure.

He had my sister.

Now, I should stop here and say that my sister does not have a single memory of our mother.

I myself have exactly one.

My memory is this: our mother is sitting on a pale mauve couch, and she's leaning forward with her arms folded, and she's saying: "That's quite a cast!"

That's it.

That's where the memory ends. We never had a pale mauve couch, and I don't know what she was talking about when she said: "That's quite a cast!"

But that's all I have, unless you count my fifteen envelopes. My sister has seventeen envelopes, but that's because she's younger.

My sister's name is Tym, pronounced Tim, and my name is Jay, pronounced Jay, and that's even though we're both girls.

In the auditorium, everyone was looking over their shoulders and over other people's shoulders, trying to see who was gasping.

Mr. Kershaw put the microphone back to his mouth and repeated the question: "You're the lucky lady, and what's your name?"

This time there was not even a gasp. There was just quiet breathing.

Beside me, Kara bit her lip and raised her eyebrows. I was sending a message to my sister: *It's Tym, Tym, all you've got to do is say your name.*

Mr. Kershaw thought he'd be funny. "Hello? Earth to Tym? Is this thing working?" He tapped the microphone against his forehead.

One or two stupid people laughed, and I sent another message, this time to Kershaw: *You already know her name. Maybe hit your head a little harder with that thing.*

"Okay, let's try this then. Can you stand up for me, Tym? It's Tym Montagne, isn't it? Can I ask you to do that?"

So there was Tym standing in her place, and everyone was staring, and Kershaw was joking: "Turns out your legs work even if your mouth doesn't seem to!"

The envelopes our mother left us are labeled with instructions, like this: To be opened on Jay's eighth birthday. Or: Only open when you turn twelve, Tym. Sometimes they contain helpful advice, such as: Don't drink coffee just before you get your legs waxed, OK? And then a year later: Don't get your legs waxed till you're older.

Other times the letters are surprising. Here's a good example. On my tenth birthday, my letter said:

> *Dear Jay,*
>
> *Happy birthday! Here's a surprise: When you and your sister were born, I gave you each a secret name. The names you have now are actually just nicknames — your secret names are on your birth certificates! I chose them by closing my eyes, opening a random page of the dictionary, and seeing where my finger landed. (Your father agreed, eventually.)*

The birth certificates are in Dad's filing cabinet.

It's up to you whether you keep your name a secret.

I hope you like it. I think it's rather lovely.

Take care, Jay, and never eat too many Smarties.

Your Loving Mother

I got my birth certificate from Dad and it turned out that my real name is Jealousy. Jealousy Anne Montagne.

I decided to keep that to myself.

So then, two years later, when it was Tym's tenth birthday, I wondered if she would get the same letter, and sure enough, there was the clang of the filing cabinet, and the next thing I knew, she was rushing in to wake me with the news.

It turned out that her real name is Timidity.

"What's your real name?" she asked, breathless. "Did you get one too?"

I explained that I could never tell, and she strangled me until she saw I meant it.

Then she sat on the floor and whispered, "Timidity."

"Look at it this way," I said. "Her finger could have landed on 'Tidbit.'"

But Tym sprang up from the floor onto the

bed, and I realized that she didn't want comfort. She wanted congratulations. Then I realized why: the name fit. Our mother had predicted her true nature.

Now in the auditorium, Tym's true nature was on display for the school. Her arms were folded tight, and she was staring up at Kershaw. "What's your topic going to be?" He grinned, and took a square of paper from his pocket.

"Okay, you know the rules of Impromptu Time, Tym, but I'll remind you! I read the topic, you have ten seconds to think, and then you speak for a full minute! You can stay where you are, or go on up to the stage if you prefer. And you can use any prop that you see. Within reason, of course. Think you can do it, Tym?"

He didn't look at her as he asked this; he looked down at the paper. "Butterflies! It's an easy one, Tym. You may even have some in your stomach there! Butterflies! There you go! Your ten-second thinking time will begin . . . now!"

My sister fluttered in her place.

Mr. Kershaw counted down from ten to one.

Then he punched the microphone at Tym, and she had to take it to protect her chest. She lifted the microphone slowly to her mouth.

There was absolute quiet.

After a few moments, Mr. Kershaw turned into a school principal. "Okay, Tym," he said, sternly. "You know there are no exceptions to Impromptu Time. It's one minute out of your life. Butterflies, Tym. Let's hear it."

I sent suggestions to Tym inside my head: *Butterflies are pretty. Butterflies can fly. A butterfly is prettier than a moth.*

But Mr. Kershaw was a comedian again, knocking on my sister's head and shouting: "Anybody in there? Hello!"

She took a deep breath and whispered, "Butterflies."

There was another long silence.

Mr. Kershaw grabbed the microphone and announced to the school: "We have a little sparrow! We have a bird in our midst! We might have better ears than birds, but we still can't hear you, little sparrow!"

At that point, Mr. Bayley stepped in.

"Actually," he called from the stage. "Actually, birds have better hearing than humans. As a rule."

Mr. Kershaw squinted up at him.

"We were just doing The Ear in my biology class," he explained, tossing his soccer ball from hand to hand. "We weren't doing Birds, but still, let me assure you, a barn owl can hear a field mouse grating cheddar from a hundred miles away. . . ."

Students talked among themselves. Tym sank slowly to her chair. Mr. Bayley shared bird trivia with the front row.

Eventually, another teacher stood up and said,

"That's great, Mr. Bayley. But I wonder if the bell's about to ring?"

Mr. Kershaw knocked on Tym's head again. "I'm not sure how you pulled that off, little sparrow!" he announced. "But know this! Next week you won't be so lucky! Next week, Impromptu Time is yours!"

The rest of the day, butterfly phrases bounced around in my head. *A butterfly used to be a caterpillar. A butterfly has six legs.* Kara pointed out that Tym would get a new Impromptu topic next week. She understood that I found it therapeutic, but she didn't want to hear any more about butterflies.

I went to the library and got more phrases: *A butterfly has an exoskeleton. Butterflies can only fly if they're warm enough. Sometimes they have to sunbathe before they can fly.*

I thought of Nero Belmonte leaning against the window in the auditorium. The sun had been lighting up his hair.

I thought of Nero's exoskeleton. I thought of Nero with giant yellow wings, hovering above me at assembly, pressing his fingers to my ears.

As soon as I got home, I called Mrs. Belmonte and asked if she needed me to babysit on the weekend.

"That's so sweet of you, Jay!" (That's what Mrs. Belmonte always says when I call.) "And it's only Tuesday too! We are going out this Saturday, but Nero has offered to stay home."

Oh, Nero.

You stole my heart, and sometimes you steal my babysitting money too.

Of course, the main reason I babysit Nero's little brothers is to get close to Nero. But if the Belmontes ever need me to babysit, it's because Nero has gone out. It's my paradox.

I told Mrs. Belmonte I'd keep Saturday free anyway, in case there was an emergency, or maybe Nero would need extra help, or whatever; then I went to find my sister.

She was doing a handstand against her mirrored wardrobe.

Tym is another paradox. She's so shy that family friends spend years believing she is mute. But when she's home with just me and Dad, she slides down the hallway in her socks, somersaults off the couch, and shouts from the middle of the kitchen: "Vot would you say if I said that I ate the last Veetabix?" before laughing like a maniac.

"So, Kara and me have a contract out on Kershaw," I said from the doorway, talking to her upside-down head. "You wanna be there when it goes down?"

Tym drummed her heels on the wardrobe door, making the mirror shake.

"Just tell me when it's done," she decided.

I sat on her bed and we discussed more reasonable options for avoiding next week's Impromptu Time. We could get Tym a disguise. She could hide in the bathrooms next Tuesday, and every Tuesday, from now on. She could drop out of school and go into witness protection.

Eventually, I said, "You know, you don't have to talk about the actual topic that he gives you if you don't want. You can talk about whatever. You just make a stupid link. Like, when I got picked last year, my topic was the ozone layer, so I said, 'The ozone layer protects us from the sun just as animal fur protects them from the wind,' and then I talked about carnivorous animals."

"Why would you want to talk about carnivorous animals?" wondered Tym. She dropped to the floor from the wardrobe and started doing push-ups. That was unexpected.

"People are going to expect you to be quiet again," I said. "You could use it as a chance to surprise them and do the opposite. You could even think of it as a chance to surprise yourself."

We looked at one another in the mirror for a moment. Taped on her mirror frame is one of our mother's letters:

> Dear Tym,
>   Happy 11th birthday! Look in the mirror often, won't you? Look in the mirror, think about who you are, and surprise yourself.
> Best wishes,
> Your Loving Mother

I got a similar letter on my eleventh birthday, but I didn't tape it to my mirror. I thought it was terrible advice: look in the mirror often. Did she want us sitting around staring at ourselves all day? Did she want us getting anorexic?

But Tym is obsessed with the letter. She thinks there must be a hidden message, and she keeps trying to decode it. Like, our mother wants us to check our appearance often to make sure we don't have bread crumbs on our cheeks. Or maybe she wants us to stare at ourselves until we see how we resemble her, and that's her way of saying she's still with us.

I stood up from the bed. "Don't even think about next week," I suggested. Then I saw my school bag lying in the hallway. I took out my biology folder and dropped it on Tym's bed. "We just did The Ear, but we did Human Reproduction a couple of weeks ago," I said. "Use that as your topic if you like. All you've got to do is make the link." She was laughing as I headed to my room, which I did without looking back, so neither of us would get embarrassed.

Later that night, I was watching TV when my dad wandered by and said, "Watching TV?"

I explained that I wasn't watching TV so much as trying to collect new landscapes for my dreams.

"Hokeydoke," said Dad, and sat down beside me on the couch.

But I was watching *Sex and Chocolate,* and as soon

as he sat down, the voice-over said, "Let's find out how kinky you really are!" and my dad said, "Hokeydoke. Night-night then," and stood up with a yawn.

My dad uses the letter "h" a lot. Often he'll say he's going to go look something hup on the hinternet in his hoffice. And don't wait hup for him, hokay? Many would find that annoying, but my sister and I are accustomed to it. It's just the way he talks.

Also, my sister was once watching the home movie of her own third birthday and the cameraman, who was my dad, says in his close-to-the-camera voice, "What's the special occasion, Tym?" And Tym says, shyly, "Hum. Hit's my birthday." Then the camera swings around to the kitchen, where our mother is doing the hokey pokey.

You can tell from the movie that Tym will turn out to be beautiful. She has the cheekbones already, and the auburn highlights and the arched eyebrows. Cheekbones? She was only three. She should have just had cheeks.

Anyway, what Tym noticed was not her eyebrows, but her use of the letter "h," as in "hum" and "hit's." And that got her excited.

"Do you think Dad talks that way now," she asked, "as a tribute to our mother? Because it's the way I used to talk when she was still around?"

I could tell Tym really wanted this to be true: that Dad held on to her baby talk to suspend Mum's hokey pokey.

But I had to be honest. "Tym," I said, "I think a lot of parents keep using their kids' words after the kids have grown up."

I gave her an example. Nero's family has an old gray station wagon, which Nero gets to use, and once, Nero's mum threw the keys to Nero's dad, so he could drive me home after babysitting. "You want to take the nu nu?" she said, as she threw them. And Nero's dad looked down at the keys and said, "But I hate the nu nu. It's such a nerdy car."

After a moment, I asked, "What's a nu nu?"

And they explained that the station wagon had been their new car when Nero was small, and they'd referred to it as "the new car," so Nero, being young and sweet, had called it "nu nu," and the name had stuck.

"That's cute," said Tym, "but kind of annoying."

"No," I explained, "it's adorable."

But, oh, Nero, it's true you are annoying.

The fact is, it was unfair to blame my biology teacher. None of my fantasies about Nero have ever come true. And you can only blame Nero for that. I swear, they are so *easy*. Do I long for him to kiss my fingertips, or to park the nu nu in an alley and embrace me? No. I don't even ask for him to speak to me.

In March, all I wanted was for him to notice a lunchbox lying on the art room floor, and kick it sideways toward me.

In April, I just wanted him to reach over and unzip the pocket of my jacket, take out the packet of M&M's (which I kept there the whole month), hold them in the palm of his hand, and put them back.

And now that it is May, I only want his fingers in my ears.

Yet I know he will never do these things. (I've never even seen a lunchbox on the art room floor, for a start.) It's not even Nero's fault, really, it's the paradox again: by thinking them up at all, I make them impossible.

Which is why I was not even really surprised when Nero said: "Hey, Jay, can I ask you something?"

I had never come close to imagining such a thing. That Nero might want to ask me something.

It was the Friday after the assembly and I was leaning against the wall outside my advanced mathematics class. Nero was heading to his intermediate class next door.

"Hey, Jay," he said, "can I ask you something?"

His sleeves were pushed up to his elbows so you could see some of his lovely exoskeleton. The sun was shining behind him, lighting up his hair.

For comic effect, I pretended to consider before I agreed. "Okay. You can ask me something."

"It's about the assembly on Tuesday."

For a quivering moment, I believed he was going to explain why he did not cross the auditorium to stand behind my chair. Maybe his fingernails were dirty.

"And how Kershaw was such a prick to your sister?" he continued. "And now he's making her do Impromptu Time again next Tuesday? Well, I just wanted to say, if she needed any help, I don't know, I could talk to her, give her advice on how to cope with Kershaw? 'Cause I know how to cope with him, see. Maybe I can somehow do her speech for her or something. Know what I'm saying?"

He was nodding and shaking his head as he talked, and every time he moved, the sun stopped lighting up his hair and blinded my eyes.

I put my hands on either side of his head and shifted it into position so it blocked the sun. I did this quite roughly.

"There," I instructed. "Keep it there."

He seemed surprised, but held his head obediently still and waited.

I regarded him.

"You realize," I said, "that my sister is half your age?"

He looked confused. "No she's not," he suggested, tentatively.

"Yes. She is." I became brisk. "She's thirteen. And you're sixteen, right? So, thirteen over sixteen, cancel the ones, that leaves three and six, and three is half of six. So she's half your age. It's advanced calculus. You'll get to it next term."

For a second, he almost fell for it.

Then he grinned, and a complicated look crossed his face—something wry, disappointed, gentle, and kind—that altogether made me want to punch him.

"I'll let her know you offered," I said, and spun on my heel.

"He's not good enough for you," Kara comforted.

But she says that about every guy I've ever loved, including Ashton Kutcher.

And this time she was wrong. I was the one who was not good enough for him. But my little sister was.

I'd never even thought of Tym as a girl before. I'd never imagined her talking to a guy; she was much too quiet. But now I remembered those cheekbones. She wouldn't need to say a word. They'd just want to look at her. And they'd talk for her.

Soon Nero would be kicking lunchboxes across floors toward my sister. He'd be unzipping her jacket pocket to take out M&M's. He'd be hooking his little fingers into her ears.

It was while I was realizing all this, sitting sadly in advanced mathematics, that my mother's mirror letter became clear.

Tym was supposed to stare at the mirror because it would teach her that, although her name might be Timidity, she was also really pretty, so that would be okay. And I was supposed to look at myself and see that I was average, maybe even strange looking, and although my name was Jealousy, well, that was exactly right. I was supposed to be jealous of my sister.

From now on, Tym would steal every boy I ever loved, without saying a word.

My destiny was all wrapped up.

Our mother had been trying to warn me.

I did not say a word to my sister throughout that sad weekend. I'm not sure she noticed.

Midnight on Monday, I woke Tym up and said, "Nero Belmonte says he can help with your speech if you want."

"Mfwuh?" She likes to sleep facedown on the pillow.

"He offered to help with your speech tomorrow."

"Nero?" She turned over. "Your Nero?" (That was respectful.)

"You'll have time before school if you get in early."

"Why would I want that?" she murmured, and fell asleep again.

I had passed on Nero's offer, just as promised.

The next day, there was a humming through the school. This is what the humming said: *We feel so sorry for Tym. And so angry with Kershaw. At least we won't get picked for Impromptu Time today. Tym will be picked. We can relax. But we feel anxious for Tym. But at least we can relax. But—.*

And so on.

At assembly, the humming became feverish, and found its way into my stomach. Beside me, Kara looked pale, and we ignored the announcements, awards, and musical displays.

When Mr. Kershaw announced, "Impromptu Time!" the auditorium breathed in sharply. He jogged across the stage, toward the stairs—but then he stopped.

Tym was standing at the bottom of the stairs.

"How about that?" twinkled Mr. Kershaw. "Our sparrow's flown to the stage! Come on up then, Tym, let's not waste any time!"

There was an interested murmuring.

It was a good start: Tym taking the initiative like that.

"She'll still have to speak," Kara pointed out.

Tym stood in the center of the stage, looking small next to Mr. Kershaw. They both faced the school. Behind them, teachers and guest speakers sat in an embarrassed-looking row.

"Right, then." Mr. Kershaw assumed his solemn voice. "No more excuses, Tym. This is something that we do every week. Nobody is exempt, and I don't want you trying to get out of—"

"Cut the crap," someone shouted. "She's standing up there, isn't she?"

A few other people shouted intelligent things like: "Yeah!"

"Hecklers!" Mr. Kershaw smiled at Tym, as if the

comments were directed at her instead of him. "Think you can cope?"

He reached into his pocket for a topic.

"The rules again," he said, closing his fist over the paper. "You can use any prop you like—"

But he stopped, because Tym had turned around and was walking to the back of the stage. She was picking up an empty chair, which was next to Mr. Bayley, and she was carrying it back to Mr. Kershaw.

"A chair?" he said. "You want to use a chair as a prop? But you don't even know what the topic is yet."

"Not the chair," she said. "You."

Then she waved a graceful hand, indicating he should sit down.

There was a brief burst of laughter and applause, along with a ripple of people saying, "What did she say?" and "What happened?" and others quickly explaining it. She'd been speaking in a quiet voice.

Tym straightened her shoulders when she heard the applause, and you could see a tiny smile.

"All right." Mr. Kershaw relaxed into the chair, and put the microphone back to his mouth. "All right, Tym, have it your way. But you're not getting out of this. What do we have here? *Pens!* It's another easy one. I'm sure you've used them to write before, and now you just have to talk about them! Ready for the count-down? Everyone, here's Tym Montagne and pens. Ten, nine, eight, seven . . ."

Tym reached out, took the microphone out of his

hand, and held it to her mouth. "Pens," she announced. There was an outbreak of relieved applause.

Then she looked around, and uneasiness returned.

She headed back to the row of teachers, while Kershaw called, "Okay, Tym, let's hear it," from his chair. But she ignored him, reached out to a clipboard that was sitting on a teacher's lap, and slid the pen from under the clip. She moved back to Kershaw's seat, pressed the pen above his ear, and spoke into the microphone: "A pen is often placed behind a nerdy person's ear."

There was more clapping and laughing, as Mr. Kershaw tried to smile with the pen behind his ear. Some of the teachers on the stage smiled, and Mr. Bayley laughed out loud.

"Actually," said Tym, retrieving the pen. "The ear can be useful for many things besides holding pens. You can use it to hold your hair back." With the pen, she pushed Mr. Kershaw's hair behind his ear. "Or to carry your ear-rings." She poked the pen at the places on his ear where earrings might be.

Kershaw started to look annoyed, but he tried to laugh along.

"The part of the ear which we see," she said, jabbing the pen at his ear again, "is called the pinna. But you'll be surprised to hear that there are things going on inside Mr. Kershaw's head."

The audience shouted with laughter while she

knocked on his head with her knuckles, a serious expression on her face. Even the teachers were laughing.

"You've got an ear canal leading to an eardrum," she continued, drumming the microphone on his head, "which you find in the middle ear, along with three tiny bones. They're the smallest bones in your body—smaller than the arm bone." She jabbed the pen at his arm. "Smaller than the leg bone." She gently kicked his leg. "Smaller than—but you get the picture. And then there's the inner ear, where you've got the cochlea and the Eustachian tube, which runs down to the nose."

She tapped him on the nose, three times, hard, with the pen.

Mr. Kershaw cleared his throat and frowned.

Tym was looking around again. Now she took the soccer ball from Mr. Bayley's lap. She threw it to Mr. Kershaw. He fumbled but managed to hold on to it.

"The cochlea," she said, gazing at him sternly, "looks nothing like that soccer ball, Mr. Kershaw. It looks like a snail!"

People had been laughing all along, but for some reason this made them hysterical.

Over the noise, Tym continued: "Before you can hear something, a noise has to be loud enough. It has to cross the threshold of hearing. But if a sound is really loud, it can break the tiny bones in your ears."

She took the soccer ball from Kershaw's lap,

returned it to Mr. Bayley, and picked up Bayley's coaching megaphone from the floor by his feet.

"Loud sounds can cross the threshold of pain. Last week, we found out that Mr. Kershaw has a low threshold of hearing. Let's test his threshold of pain!"

And she pressed the megaphone up to his ear and shouted: "CAN YOU HEAR ME NOW?!"

His mouth fell open, he ducked away, and she ducked to keep up with him. The entire school was shrieking with laughter, and Tym kept shouting, while Mr. Kershaw tried to escape.

I looked over at Nero, leaning against the window as usual, and he was looking right at me. He was shaking his head and grinning. And suddenly a question jumped into my head: did Nero ask if he could help my sister because he wanted to be my friend? And after the assembly, would we talk about Tym, kind of like parents being proud, and would I say, "Turned out she didn't need your help," and would he say, "Oh, yeah, I know," and would I say, "We should drive around in your nu nu for a while, and think about how strange it is that Tym got to be so brave"?

And then I thought of something else: I thought of what our mother might have meant with her mirror letters.

Maybe she meant that mirrors turn things around, reflect them in reverse. Maybe she wanted Timidity to look at a mirror and realize she was actually Brave.

And maybe I should see Jealousy there, and turn it into something like Pride.

All around me people were laughing at Tym's jokes, and I wanted to stand up and shout, "That's my little sister!"

As the laughter subsided, Tym dropped the megaphone and put the microphone back to her mouth. "And to conclude," she said, straight-faced. "Some day you might want to put your finger into a friend's ear. But never, ever use a pen."

Then she aimed the pen at Mr. Kershaw's ear and chased him across the stage.

WHY I HIT MY BOYFRIEND
Dyan Sheldon

When Aidan McClusky asked me out the first time, I thought he'd made a mistake. You know, that he'd been temporarily blinded or got hit in the head in a soccer game, or something like that.

I said, "You what?"

Aidan said, "You want to go to a movie sometime?"

I looked over my shoulder, just in case he was talking to some so-popular-I-should-be-illegal girl behind me. There was no one there.

I better explain that Aidan McClusky was eat-your-heart-out gorgeous, and one of the hottest boys at Pulaski High, if not the hottest. There wasn't a cheerleader, potential prom queen, or ultimate babe in the entire school who wouldn't have given up her clothes allowance for at least six months to go out with him. He was totally A-list. Which is why I was a little confused. The most I was was B-list. Bottom of B. Aidan and I sat next to each other in English and we were friendly, but the fact that we joked about the food in the cafeteria and the principal's hair implants didn't mean anything. He was friendly to the Z-list geek who sat on the other side of him in English, too. Aidan was a friendly kind of guy.

"Well?" Aidan looked at his watch in an exaggerated way. "What do you say, Mimi? I was thinking of going within the next week, not the next year."

I laughed. "Sure," I said. "That'd be great."

"Maybe he lost a bet," said Bethany.

"Thanks," I said. "It's times like these when you realize how important it is to have a best friend."

"You know what I mean," said Bethany. "Aidan McClusky's dated practically every seriously popular girl in school at least once."

"What are you saying? That he's run out of popular girls, so he had to ask me? Or that he's a serial dater?"

"I'm not saying anything. I'm just stating a fact." Bethany shrugged. "You know . . . I wouldn't get my hopes up—you know, for anything to come of it."

It had never happened before, but it occurred to me that Bethany might be jealous. The boys she dated weren't exactly the kind to make Orlando Bloom consider plastic surgery.

"What hopes? We're just going to the movies, not getting engaged."

When he took me home after the movie, Aidan said it was the best date he'd ever had. I said, "Me too." Then he said the soccer team had a game on Saturday afternoon. Aidan was the captain and the star player. Aidan said, "It'd bring me good luck if you were there."

I was supposed to go shopping with Bethany, but I said I'd go.

I asked Bethany to come with me. "We can go shopping after it's over."

"Yeah, right. If Aidan doesn't have other ideas." I could tell from her voice that Bethany was making her sucking-a-lemon face. "Anyway, I don't like soccer any more than you do."

I said I didn't know if I liked it or not because I'd never really seen a game.

"Well, here's your big chance," said Bethany.

After the game Aidan did have other ideas. He invited me to go for pizza with the team. "You're the one who brought us luck. You're practically an honorary member."

I sat next to him and smiled a lot and pretended I understood what they were talking about.

When he drove me home Aidan said, "I should never've brought you along with all those guys. I saw the way they were looking at you."

I didn't think they were looking at me at all. The only time they technically took their eyes off their food was when they were illustrating a play with pieces of crust and an olive.

Aidan gazed into my eyes. "You don't know the effect you have on guys, Mimi."

Except for the time I walked into Craig Ziggy in the cafeteria and knocked his tray out of his hands, and it hit Foxy Daniels in the head and a fight broke out, I didn't think I had any effect on boys.

"You're not like the other girls I've dated. They

were always flirting with other guys." Aidan kissed the tip of my nose. "Stay as sweet as you are."

That was my plan.

After that we didn't make dates anymore; we were officially going out.

"He's been hurt in love," I reported to Bethany. "Girls are always breaking his heart."

Bethany smirked. "And how could they do that when he never dates anyone more than twice?"

"You don't know him. Aidan's really very sensitive. He may come over as megaconfident and sure of himself, but deep down he's really insecure." It made me want to protect him.

But it didn't make Bethany want to protect him. She rolled her eyes. "Yeah, right. Him and Tom Cruise."

I smiled at myself in a passing window. "And anyway, the serial dating thing's all in the past." Just the thought made me feel like I'd fallen into a heated pool. "As of last night he's officially going out with me."

Bethany looked more like she'd fallen into mud. "Oh yeah? And what brought about this astounding transformation?"

I couldn't help feeling a little smug. "He met the right girl."

"I never see you anymore," complained Bethany.

"What are you talking about?" Aidan had practice, so she and I were walking home from school together. I wasn't invited along anymore to cheer on the soccer team because Aidan said my presence threw the other guys off their game. Mainly we just hung out at his house or mine by ourselves. Aidan said he didn't like to share me. "You see me every day."

Bethany kicked a stone off the pavement. "In school. You and four hundred other people."

I laughed. "Oh, come on . . . you know what it's like when you first start dating someone."

Bethany's laugh was a little on the snorting donkey side. "No, but I'm finding out."

"Oh, come on, Beth . . ." I could feel myself blush. "I think maybe I'm falling in love."

Bethany raised one eyebrow in a what's-that-fork-doing-in-my-makeup-case kind of way. "Is that what you call it? Love?"

"Yes." I nodded, slowly but firmly. It was the first time I'd used the "L" word. "Yes, that's what I call it."

"It could be mistaken for something else," said Bethany.

I didn't bother to ask her what.

"Lighten up, will you?" I gave her a playful poke. "It's just that it takes a lot of work to build a relationship."

"You could build a house in less time," said Bethany.

I laughed. "Hey, I've got an idea. Why don't we do something tomorrow night? Bowling or something?"

She came to a stop and eyed me suspiciously. "What about Aidan? I thought Friday was your night to watch horror videos with him. Don't tell me you're going to pass up an evening of blood, gore, and saliva to go bowling with me."

"He's hanging out with his friends."

Bethany sighed. "I should've known."

Aidan gave me a kiss. "I'll call you later from Brad's," he promised. "It could be a long night."

"I won't be home." I kissed him back. "I'm seeing Bethany."

"Well, bring your cell phone. You can stop yakking with her long enough to talk to me for a few minutes, can't you?"

I told him we were going bowling. The bowling alley forbids cell phones. The manager says serious bowlers don't want to lose their concentration because a nearby phone starts playing "Bohemian Rhapsody."

Aidan said, "Bowling?" His smile was suddenly a lot less warm and friendly than a boa constrictor's. "Who with?"

"Nobody. Just me and Beth."

"You and Bethany are going bowling by yourselves?" The boa constrictor had slithered onto an ice floe. "Are you serious?"

"Of course I'm serious." The way he was reacting, you'd think I said we were going on a turkey shoot. "We used to go all the time."

"I bet you did."

There was something in his tone that made me

feel like I'd been bitten, but I didn't show it. "What's that supposed to mean?" I teased.

Aidan didn't so much as smile. "I'm not getting at you, Mi. But everybody knows what a flirt Bethany is."

"They do?" It was news to me.

"Look, I know she's your best friend and everything, but the only reason Bethany'd go bowling is to pick up boys."

This time I really laughed. "Bethany's been bowling since she was five. Her mother's got trophies."

"I don't care if Bethany was born with a bowling ball in her hand and her mom's an Olympic champ. I'm telling you what I know." He wrapped his arms around me and leaned his head on mine. "I don't like you going out with her. She's not a good influence."

"But . . ."

"You know how I feel about you, Mi. I—I really— well, you know—I really like you. It'd drive me crazy to think you were hanging out with other guys."

It felt like my blood was bubbling. He'd almost said the "L" word! If my heart beat any faster, it would implode. Now definitely wasn't the time to have a fight.

"And you know how I feel about you . . ." I nuzzled against him. "I don't want to upset you—not ever."

"I know you don't." He gave me a squeeze. "So I'll phone you at home from Brad's tonight, okay?"

I said I'd be waiting.

* * *

Never mind that I could've built a house for all the work I put into building my relationship with Aidan; I could've built Rome. I promised that I would never upset him, and I meant it. It became my mission in life to always make him happy. That's what love is. Making someone else happy. I was only sixteen, but I knew that much. I'd read the books, heard the songs, and seen the movies.

I used to have a lot of male friends at school, but I stopped hanging out with them or saying anything more than "Hi" or "How's it going?" because Aidan didn't like it.

"We're just friends," I said the first time Aidan got all bent out of shape because he saw me talking to Jared Bell.

"You're so naïve," Aidan told me. "Can't you see he's after you?"

I said that he wasn't. Jared and I had been friends since grade school.

"Then maybe you're not naïve," said Aidan. "Maybe you're just like all the rest."

I didn't want to be like all the rest.

So, because I didn't want to be like all the rest, I pretty much stopped going out with Bethany and my other friends. Aidan didn't trust them.

I stopped wearing skirts because Aidan said my skirts were all too short and would give guys the wrong idea.

I stopped running when I was late for a class

because Aidan said my boobs bounced so much that everybody looked at me.

I kept my eyes on the ground when I was out with Aidan because he always thought I was looking at other boys.

It was all pretty exhausting, but I was happy. I was in love. What was there not to be happy about?

And then Bethany's cousin, Josie, came for the weekend.

I'd known Josie for as long as I'd known Bethany. Before Josie's family moved away, the three of us were always together. Which made her one of my oldest friends.

"What do you mean, you're not coming out with us?" said Bethany. "It's all set." The idea was that we'd go out for pizza and then have a sleepover at Bethany's. Just like old times.

"I can't," I said. "I'm supposed to be seeing Aidan."

"Well, can't you not see him for one night? He lives three miles from you, not three hundred like Josie. She's expecting you to be there. What am I supposed to tell her? That you're in love, so you don't mingle with the peasants anymore?"

"But I promised."

Bethany cocked one eyebrow in a so-what way. "I don't think it's legally binding, Mi. Just tell him something came up."

I couldn't do that.

"He'll be hurt that I'd rather spend time with you guys than with him."

"Hurt?" Bethany laughed as though I'd made the best joke ever. "Why would he be hurt? You just want to hang out with your friends. He hangs out with his, doesn't he?"

I couldn't explain.

"Are you sure you're in love, or have you had a lobotomy?" Bethany studied my face like she was looking for clues. "Don't you want to see Josie?"

"Of course I do." I did.

"Well, think about it," said Bethany. "You can always change your mind."

It was Aidan who changed his mind.

"The team's going out for a victory celebration," Aidan informed me on Saturday afternoon. "Since we've won every game this season so far."

I said, "Oh. That sounds terrific."

"It should be fun."

I smiled. "So, where are you going?"

"The coach got the department van so he's driving us all to The Steak Out."

The Steak Out's one of those gigantic hunks of meat and all-you-can-eat salad bar places. It's miles out of town. And as soon as I realized that, I heard Bethany say, *He goes out with his friends, doesn't he?* And I decided I'd go out with my friends too. It would be fun. Just like old times.

Aidan put his arms around me. "I'll call you like I always do."

I said, "Great."

"For God's sake," whispered Bethany while we waited for Josie to run into the candy store for some gum. "What's wrong with you?"

"Nothing."

"Yes, there is. You're all tense and distracted. And you almost walked into a tree back there."

"It's because of the rain." This was a lie. I almost walked into the tree because I forgot for a few minutes that I didn't have to walk with my eyes on the ground. "I can hardly see. And I'm not tense and distracted." But I was. What if we ran into Aidan after all? I felt like I was wanted by the government and that someone from the FBI was waiting around the next corner to catch me. But I wasn't going to tell Bethany that. It was one thing thinking it, but even I knew that saying it out loud would make it sound really stupid. "I just miss Aidan, that's all."

"Miss Aidan?" Bethany stared at me as if she'd just seen a Klingon. "What are you talking about, 'Miss Aidan'? He's gone for a meal with the soccer team, not to war."

"I know . . . but . . . you know . . . I'm not used to being out without him."

"Well, you used to be. You used to be just dandy without him." Bethany linked an arm in mine. "Why don't you try to relax and enjoy yourself, Mi? Forget about Aidan till the morning." She squeezed my arm. "He has no trouble forgetting about you for a night."

"That's not true. He always calls me when he's out with his friends."

"Not tonight he doesn't." Before I could stop her, Bethany snatched my cell phone out of my pocket. She turned it off and stuck it in her bag. "Tonight you're incommunicado."

Maybe it was because Bethany took the phone from me like that, but right away I started to relax. Because even though Aidan probably wouldn't call till he got home, if he did call while we were at the restaurant, I would've felt I had to answer it. And if I'd answered it, he would've known that I wasn't in my room doing my history homework like I'd said I would be. I'd take the phone back when we got to Bethany's, and when he called I'd go to the bathroom to talk to him and he'd never know the difference.

Once I relaxed it didn't take me long to get used to it being like old times. You know, not making sure I didn't accidentally glance at anyone. Not worrying that my boobs jiggled when I laughed. Smiling back at the waiter. Not having to pretend to be interested in the complexities of soccer passes. That kind of thing. It's like when you buy a new pair of shoes that need to be broken in. You hobble around for days and days until you don't really notice that you're limping and your toes hurt. And then you take them off and put your old sneakers on, and right away you feel so good you forget how bad you felt ten minutes ago.

It took us ages to get through our meal because we were talking and laughing so much. I couldn't remember the last time I had so much fun.

We stopped to get snacks and a couple of movies on the way home. We were planning to stay up all night.

Bethany's folks were just walking out the door when we got to the house.

"Mimi, you still live around here?" joked Mrs. Parrish. "It's ages since we've seen you. I thought you'd moved away."

"Well, as happy as we are to see you, we're not staying here with three nonstop talkers and shriekers," declared Mr. Parrish. "We're going to the fights to get some peace and quiet."

Mrs. Parrish rolled her eyes at Bethany. "We'll be at the Menczers' playing cards, honey. I left the number on the fridge."

"Put the alarm on after we go," said Mr. Parrish. "You know how to set the new system, don't you, Beth?"

Bethany's dad is always waiting to be robbed. He changes his security systems the way other people rotate their tires. The old alarm was supposed to be totally foolproof, but it kept going off for no reason, so now he'd gotten a new one. Bethany says the only place her dad would feel really safe is inside the White

House, and even then he'd be checking every door and window all the time to make sure they were locked.

Bethany groaned. "Oh, Dad . . ."

"You can't be too careful nowadays," said Mr. Parrish.

About halfway through the first movie, we called an intermission. Josie went to get the pillows and blankets to turn the TV room into our bedroom, and Bethany and I went to the kitchen to make popcorn and nachos.

I was still grating the cheese and Bethany was still looking for the popcorn when Josie came rushing in. She was gibbering.

"For God's sake, Jo. Slow down," I ordered. "I can't understand a word you're saying."

Josie took a few deep breaths and started again. "There's someone trying to get into the house. I saw him prowling around the back from the bedroom."

"Oh please . . ." Bethany emerged from the cabinet with the popcorn in her hand. "I can't believe you listen to my dad. You know what he's like. He's the man who called the cops because there was a raccoon in the attic and he thought it was a burglar."

"This time it's not a raccoon," Josie insisted. "I'm telling you, there's a guy trying to break in. He was at the windows. We've got to do something. Quick."

But Bethany lives with the Man Who Cried Wolf and was used to this sort of crisis. She calmly put oil in the pot. "There's nothing to panic about. The alarm's on, remember? It's even got lights. If he sets that off, it'll give him the scare of his life."

I said, "Is it?"

Bethany looked at me. She was still trying to act calm but her eyes were wide. "Oh my God . . . My dad's going to kill me! I never put it on, did I?"

"What'd I tell you?" Josie turned toward the door. "I'll call the cops."

"Don't bother. They won't come unless they happen to be passing by. The raccoon was the fourth time in six months." Bethany took a flashlight from one of the drawers. "I'll go put the alarm on, and then I'll call the 'rents. Jo, you check all the doors and windows up here. Mimi, you take the basement." She handed me the flashlight. "You'll need this; the light's not working. They did something to the circuit when they put in the alarm."

Beth, Jo, and I had a clubhouse in the basement when we were little, but I hadn't been down there in years. I went quietly and carefully down the stairs. I was really scared, but I was cautious. The light from the kitchen was enough for me to see my way down the stairs, but when I reached the bottom I was pretty much swallowed by darkness. I turned on the flashlight. It didn't work.

I stood there for a few seconds trying to remember where everything was. The Parrishes' basement was once an apartment, but it hadn't been used for that since they moved in. The room straight in front of me was the one we'd used for our clubhouse. There were two more rooms off of that. One is the old kitchen, which is just a storeroom now, and the other is where Mr. Parrish keeps his pool table. Each room has one small window. The sound of the rain echoed through the cellar. I made my way to where I remembered the first window being. As far as I could tell without the advantage of sight, it seemed to be shut tight.

I turned and went back past the stairs.

I was just about to open the door to the poolroom when I heard something drop to the floor in the old kitchen. My first thought was that it was Mr. Parrish's raccoon, who'd been forced to relocate. My second thought was that it was something bigger than a raccoon. And wearing shoes. I held my breath. Oh, if only Mr. Parrish was as efficient at making sure the cellar windows were all shut and locked as he was at being paranoid.

Somewhere in my frozen brain I knew what I should do next. Someone a lot dumber than a goldfish would've known what to do: run upstairs, lock the basement door behind me, and call the police.

But I didn't do that.

I was so scared that for a couple of seconds or a couple of minutes I just stood there, my heart chugging away like one of those old-fashioned locomotives. I might as well have been cemented to the spot.

It wasn't until I heard someone fumbling for the door that I finally moved. I wasn't really thinking, but I knew it was too late for me to start charging up the stairs in the dark. I wasn't even sure where the staircase was anymore. But I knew where the old kitchen was. It was straight ahead. I went toward it. I crouched down so whoever it was wouldn't feel me breathing in his face, and as he stepped through the door, I hauled off and whacked him in the thighs with the flashlight.

There was a bloodcurdling scream of pain.

I guess my aim was a little off.

"Mimi!" Bethany shouted from the top of the stairs. "Mimi! Are you all right?"

"I'm fine," I called back. "Bring a flashlight that works. I got the burglar."

"What happened?" Josie peered over the banister into the dark. "Did you kill him?"

The burglar stopped moaning long enough to shout back, "No, she didn't kill me."

I said, "Aidan?" I couldn't have been more surprised if it *had been* a raccoon wearing shoes. I guess I should've known, really, but I'd been having such a good time that I'd completely forgotten about him. I hadn't even taken my cell phone back from Bethany.

"You know, I'll probably never have children now," he groaned.

I said, "Aidan? Aidan, what are you doing here? We thought you were a burglar."

"No kidding."

Bethany came thundering down the stairs with Josie right behind her.

"Good God!" Bethany shone her bike light on the crumpled figure by the door. "It's Aidan McClusky. What are you doing in my house?"

Aidan glared at me. "It's all your fault."

It was my fault because when he couldn't get me on my cell phone, he rang my mother and she told him I was spending the night with Beth.

"I thought you were up to something," said Aidan.

I just stood there staring at him like I'd never seen him before. "I *was* up to something. I was making nachos."

"You know what I mean." He glared some more. "I thought you were having a party. You know, with guys."

"So you followed me here and broke into the Parrishes' house?"

"I wanted to catch you in the act."

Yesterday I probably would've thought that was a perfectly reasonable thing to say. It wasn't any less reasonable than "I don't want you to see your friends" or "I don't want you to make eye contact with any other boy." But now, standing there in Bethany's basement, my heart still pounding from the heavy dose of fear it'd had, it didn't seem reasonable at all.

"Why don't we all go upstairs?" suggested Bethany. "I guess you two want to be alone to talk."

If Aidan had come through the door like a normal person, things would have been different. But he came through the window. All this time I'd thought his possessiveness meant that he loved me—but all it meant was that he was nuts.

"We have nothing to talk about." I said this really calmly. "Aidan's just leaving."

"If I go now, that's it, Mimi. I'm not coming back."

I figured that was the best news I'd heard in weeks.

FIFTY PERCENT
Irina Reyn

Right after I ripped open the envelope that would decide where I could go to college, my parents said they wanted to talk to me.

"We want to talk to you," they said, and I was certain they knew. They knew the contents of that envelope, the numbers that revealed only a rudimentary understanding of mathematics and would rip all picture-perfect, leafy campuses out of my grasp. No doubt they could read the print on the return address; the SATs blazoned across the corner in large capital letters. I was in a wretched mood.

My parents sat stiffly on the couch, Cheshire smiles radiating on their faces. These were expressions I was not used to seeing.

"I know you are wondering how I did on my SATs." I began the speech that I imagined would wipe those foreign smiles off their faces. They looked at each other, as if raking their mental Webster's for the vocabulary word "SAT." "But don't worry, I can take them over again."

"Take what over?" my father said.

My mother blurted out, "No, we wanted to talk to you about something else." *Something something brother or sister something something you always wanted one something something next summer.* There was a long pause as I did the math on my fingers, to make sure I did not miscalculate. So that meant I would have a sibling and he or she would be born when I was almost . . . seventeen? Were they kidding?

Sure, I'd always wanted an *older* brother or sister. At seven, I wished for a companion who would immigrate to the United States with me, who would have my back in school when the other kids were mean to me, a clueless Russian girl. I fantasized about a sister who would play the male Barbie to my female Barbie (I had no Ken dolls, so poor Barbie was forced to play both roles), whose Strawberry Shortcake would rest alongside mine, who would let my Hungry Hippo gobble up all the marbles.

When I became a teenager, my sibling fantasy was tailored to a newfound interest in boys. My imaginary brother would bring his buddies, all the cute and popular boys at school, home where I would offer them freshly squeezed lemonade in an outfit easily mistaken for Madonna's, complete with lacy gloves and a bandanna tied rakishly across my forehead.

Of course, I understood that an older brother might be hard for my parents to pull off, but in those imaginary forays, I never expected my forty-year-old mother to come home and announce that I was going to have a sister a year before I graduated from high school.

* * *

"My sister." It sounded weird on my lips, like I had acquired some kind of extra limb or diabetes. It had never been a resonant word in my vocabulary. She could have been mine, and this became a joke in our household. As if I were a pregnant teenager who handed my baby over to my mother to raise. Ha ha.

When she arrived at the beginning of August, my sister was a dark, blurry thing wrapped in a thick blanket. My parents unwrapped her as though she were a souvenir from one of their vacations. Meet your sister Elizabeth, they said. Upon closer inspection, she was even more foreign than I'd imagined—olive skin, patches of black hair splattered on her head and body, tight, scrunched lids that would eventually unveil large brown eyes. I was fair-skinned, blue-eyed, and light-haired, while this creature was an exotic Gypsy child.

It was my senior year in high school. There was the school play to act in, college applications to worry about, and of course, the prom. I found myself marveling as social structures broke down and popular people began to mix with the rest of the crowd as though they realized their reign was coming to an end forever. Even our teachers appeared different— more enthusiastic, respectful—prowling the front of the room, cramming ideas into our heads as if we were actually on the brink of adulthood.

At home, my sister cried. She cried while I was filling out applications, typing my college essays, and discussing with one of my girlfriends my chances with Andy, a cute lead singer of a band. Elizabeth cried when I came home with a gift from Andy, a Billy Joel tape I played every night for a week. She cried when Andy asked another girl to the prom after raging at my football clumsiness in gym class. She cried when I decided to go to Rutgers, a college an hour away from home, and she cried when I decided to go to the prom, wearing an aerodynamic black and white dress, with one of my best male friends.

I would go to her room and stare at her while she was asleep. Why did she have to cry so much? This was not what I'd imagined a sister would be like. When would she be old enough to borrow clothes from? When would she be old enough to discuss with me my high school disappointments and boys and why they did what they did? I wanted to tell her that I was proud of being in the school play, and that I had no idea what I wanted to do with my life. I wanted to chat about the color pink—was it better for my pale complexion or her duskier one?

Throughout my meditations, she never opened an eyelid, so I imagined her silently answering me: "Yes, you can borrow my bunny, Frances, any time you want." "Don't worry, it will get better in college— you'll have friends, boyfriends, new experiences." "Boys appear strange, but in the end, they are not so different from us; they just show their emotions differently." "Good job in that play—you made a believable Jamaican maid." "Be an English major and decide later." "Pink is really better on your skin. I look good in darker colors."

Sometimes, I looked down at her and hoped for our future. Other times, I looked down and didn't like her one bit. My parents no longer had any time for me. As an only child, I was used to being at the vortex of their concentration and now, at this juncture in my life, I needed it more than ever. But they had little time to consider where I would be going to college or to help pick out my prom dress or even to look at my report cards. They were busy and exhausted with the baby, whose demands were swallowing all their time and vigor. Surely, this was a phase I might have gone through if her arrival had come when I was two or three or five—but at seventeen, to be jealous of my sister? Preposterous.

My friends sympathized, but my concerns were as foreign to them as the problems on TV Afterschool Specials.

"Come out for ice cream," they offered. "We're all meeting at Friendly's." We stood on a street corner up to our ankles in the last snow of high school, inhaling the faint pear scent of spring. We stamped our boots and blew on our mittens, shifting from one foot to the other—to the left lay Friendly's and its warm, brightly lit coziness, intimate girl conversations, and tall

Reese's Peanut Butter Cup sundaes; to the right lay my house with a cranky, sleep-deprived mother and a wailing baby.

"Nah, gotta babysit," I said, making a pained face and heading for home. My resentment grew.

"That's messed up," a girlfriend said as she walked home with me. "I can't imagine having a sister now." Then her voice shifted from funereal to upbeat as she confided in me about a stocky, thick-jawed boy who liked her. "He's cute, right? I should maybe see what happens, right?"

"Yeah, he's cute," I said, encouraging, but silently, deeply envious. Her life was so carefree, while I had responsibilities tossed onto my shoulders through no will of my own. Even if I could get a boy to like me, I probably wouldn't have time to see him.

At home, my mother was at the changing table, a towel thrown over her shoulder. My sister wriggled around, her feet poised in the air, her bare butt bouncing against the mattress, her pudgy, dimpled hands swinging from side to side like an orchestra conductor's. My mother was laughing, pretending to eat my sister's stomach, nibbling on toes and heels, tolerating the facial battering by my sister's feet. I made my presence known. My mother looked up from my sister and her expression changed, to something adult, something that smacked of obligations.

"Great, glad you're home. Can you run out for a new pack of diapers?" I backed out of the room and the cooing noise returned. "Who's Mama's favorite baby?" I heard her say.

On the walk to CVS, I surprised myself with my tears. I'm not a child, I thought, so why am I so jealous? I left the store grasping an enormous, unwieldy box of Pampers, while other customers smiled. Did they think the diapers were for *my* baby? I longed to be my sister, with the years of fun still ahead of her: going on play dates, crayoning stick figures with poufy, polka-dotted skirts, gluing trunks on elephants, watching Saturday-morning cartoons while clutching a beloved frayed, stuffed rabbit in her fingers. I did not want to pick a major or do my own laundry or get a job to pay for future sundaes. I wanted to sit on a blanket all day and play with pretty, colorful shapes.

But high school graduation came anyway and before I knew it, I was wearing a bright red robe and hat and accepting a rolled-up certificate. After the ceremony, my family waited to take me out to lunch at a local diner. I looked around at my now ex-classmates. They were surrounded by older brothers and younger sisters with flowers in their hands. Their sisters squealed, "Congratulations!" and their brothers stood around quietly but proudly, drawing circles in the gravel with their sneakers. My sister was snoozing away in her carriage, dreaming of unicorns or rainbows or happy polar bears, oblivious to this monumental event in my life.

* * *

I left the house for good when my sister turned a year old. From then on, in her eyes, I became a visitor, an auntlike figure whose sudden appearances changed the atmosphere of her predictable surroundings. When I came home from college to visit, my parents devoted the weekend to me. In her room, my sister sulked, the warm yellow glow of their attention faded for the time being.

Since my parents wanted me to be close to my sister, they often left me in charge of her for an evening. We would play a few games, my sister glaring at me suspiciously, wondering when "her" parents would finally get back. We would watch *Barney* together, she sitting in front of the television screen cross-legged with a cup of warm milk, and me on the couch with textbooks, studying for midterms.

From time to time, she would lisp "More milk" or "Barney," or she would just start to cry—long, heaving, inconsolable sobs. When my parents did get home, I would run to greet them at the door, breathing in the outdoor cold emanating from their coats, relieved that they were about to take over the tough job of entertaining a toddler.

As the years went by, I channeled my jealousy into the persona of strict parent. Since my sister took advantage of my parents' exhaustion by pressing for late bedtimes, gorging on television and eating finicky, carbohydrate-filled meals, I tried to be the disciplinarian. Observing my parents as pushovers produced a stew of bitterness and condescension within me.

"Lights out," I would bark at her doodling form clad in cotton pajamas.

"Why do I have to?" she would whine. If she expected more leniency from me, she would soon learn that I was unyielding. I still remembered being in bed by nine o'clock; no *Dukes of Hazzard,* no questions asked.

"Because I said so!" I turned off the light, watching as her drawing pad slipped to the floor and she pulled the covers over herself, defeated and angry.

My parents joked that under my reign, my sister lived in fear—her broccoli would get eaten, the television would be turned off. It was the only way I knew to relate to her. But clearly, it was no fun for either of us.

"Liza! Come say hello to your sister," my mother would call when I returned home for the weekend, a bag of laundry in tow. After a while, when we were sitting at the kitchen table with mugs of tea, my sister would finally enter the room.

"Do we have any cereal?" she would ask my mother, her hand already poking around the biscuit region of the cupboard.

"Can't you see Irina is here?" my mother would remind her. My sister would skim by me with a half-hearted pat on my back on her way to obtain milk for

145

her cereal. Before she shut her door, we could hear the cheerful music of Nickelodeon emanating from her room. A part of me was ashamed—despite so many more years of insight, I felt able to offer her little more than she offered me.

"You know, if you have any questions and you don't want to ask Mom . . . ," I began one night, sitting on the edge of her bed, trying out my best conspiratorial voice in an effort to remind us both that I was a sibling—not a parent, and not the enemy.

My sister appeared to think, crinkling her nine-year-old nose and staring up at me from the depths of her pillows. "I know," she said at last, jerking up to a sitting position. "I would ask Grandpa!" I nodded. The orange bear alarm clock by her bed said ten o'clock. An hour later, I still saw the telltale strip of light beneath her door, but I didn't have the heart to demand that she turn it off.

When my sister started junior high, I decided to tag along with my parents to her open house. We strolled the halls of the school with my sister, meeting her teachers and reading the students' work on the walls. My parents had moved to New Jersey from New York when I was in high school, so it was not a familiar environment to me. But one of my sister's instructors recognized me at once; she had been my high school geometry teacher all those years ago. A compact, energetic woman in her fifties, she grabbed my hand, gushing with memories, swearing I had been one of her very best students.

"You're a very lucky little girl, Elizabeth," she said. "To have such a smart sister. And imagine, I never connected your last names at all, isn't that funny?" My sister looked up at me, a newfound respect in her eyes, as if our worlds had intersected for the first time.

On the wall, we found her assignment hanging among all the others. It was a timeline of her life. At 0, my sister had planted her own birth and what followed afterward: to the right was a bright, compressed series of events—a memorable birthday party at +5, a vacation to Cancún at +10. But all the way to the left, almost off the edge of the green construction paper, I found "My sister is born" at -17. Since our own timelines always begin at 0, it felt unsettling to be located at -17 of someone else's. But at least I was there. I stood staring at the timeline, taking deep breaths before the proof of my existence in my sister's life.

* * *

It probably wasn't easy for Liza to grow up under the shadow of a sister whose childhood imperfections were long forgotten. To her, my parents made me out to be the ideal child, who made straight A's (truth: not really), who helped my mother with housework (truth: once in a while, if I was in the mood), who enjoyed going to museums and other cultural events (truth: if I was promised the restaurant of my choice afterward), and read voraciously (truth: OK, that was the truth, actually; I was a big geek). How could my sister compete with this ideal image?

I didn't dispel those myths either. Last year, during my sister's bat mitzvah, a man was interviewing guests with a video camera. "Say something to Elizabeth," he said, shoving a microphone into my hands. Behind him, Liza's friends were hopping around on the dance floor at the command of an ebullient DJ. I faced the camera and no words came to my mind. Do I go mushy or funny? On the spot, I opted for funny.

"My dear sister, if you accomplish even fifty percent of what I've accomplished in life, you will be very lucky," I said, mugging. The cameraman laughed and moved on. Later at home, my sister watched and rewatched her video, pressing Pause during my speech.

"What's up with that?" my sister asked, straight-faced. I shrugged. *Sorry, it was all I could think of at the moment.* For months afterward, my family tormented me. "Fifty percent!" They would sputter pieces of food and break into a whole new round of laughter. My sister joined in the fun; she was learning to joke around with me.

The closer she got to becoming a teenager, the more she started coming to me with questions. "How long did you have your braces on?" she asked, hesitantly at first, a new band of metal gleaming in her mouth.

"Six years," I told her.

"I'm supposed to have them on for three," she announced, proudly, and then after hardly a pause, "When did you get your glasses?" Soon the questions would tumble out in a rapid procession: "When did you have your first kiss?" "How did you like high school?" "Did you do as badly in gym as Mom says?" On her bookshelf, I spied my high school yearbook. She had pored over it, reading the inscriptions ("I didn't really get to know you, but good luck in college!") and possibly even seeing pictures of Andy, the boy who never really liked me at all.

It was around that time that I realized I had to quit playing the parental role and start having fun with my sister. She is fourteen now, old enough to trade make-up and boy stories with, and even, I am happy to say, share clothes. Last August, on one of my visits back home, the two of us went to the mall and returned home to order Chinese food and hunker down before the *MTV Music Awards*.

"He's hot," my sister said, pointing her fork at Usher in dark shades, her mouth stuffed with chicken and broccoli. "He has a six-pack." I could see what she meant, and I agreed; he was hot. As we slurped our sodas, dangling our feet off the couch, we swapped opinions on Ashlee and Jessica, Beyoncé and Evanescence.

* * *

Since my sister did not have the benefit of my era's teen heartthrobs, I introduced her to River Phoenix, the beautiful actor from my childhood who starred in movies like *Stand by Me* and *Running on Empty,* and who died tragically young. He now serves as my sister's computer screen saver. She has become a groupie, watching any of his movies she can get her hands on. She even added her thoughts to his memorial fan Web site. Because of me, she has seen *The Breakfast Club, Pretty in Pink, Lucas,* and all the great teen movies of the 1980s. Since the eighties are back in style, she seems pretty cool to her friends, with her large database of retro movie knowledge.

The more we hang out, the more our jealousies dissolve. We've both been writing novels, and we wonder whose book will come out first. But she has other things to do, like make it through high school and keep up her grades. Just a week ago, she received her class picture. In it, she looks so mature, her dark brown hair long and sleek—no braces or glasses in sight. She wears a black crewneck top and a tiny black leather necklace; I can't believe she's already fourteen.

"Write something," I said, recalling my own high school traditions, when we inscribed one another's wallet-sized class pictures. She thought for a minute and scrawled something on the back. Then my parents came into the room and we turned our attention to planning Thanksgiving dinner. I stuffed the picture in my wallet without reading it. Only days later, back in my own apartment, 300 miles from New Jersey, I remembered that I hadn't read my sister's inscription. I opened my wallet and slipped out the picture. On the back of her ninth-grade photo, in which she is only two years younger than I was when I found out she would be entering my life, my sister had written, "Fifty percent of what you've accomplished wouldn't be so bad."

TEST YOUR JEALOUSY QUOTIENT
Reed Tucker

As long as humans have been on the earth, jealousy has been with us. It even made one of the Ten Commandments: "Thou shalt not covet thy neighbor's Prada." Maybe it wasn't quite worded like that, but you get the idea.

And as long as magazines have existed, quizzes have been with us. They let us know how into us our crush really is, and how much like our favorite celebrities we are (whatever the point of that is).

Are you a jealous type? This quiz will explain all.

1. To your surprise, you land the lead in the school play, much to the dismay of the president of the drama club, who also tried out for the part. You:

a. Pat her on the back and assure her she'll get it next time.

b. Throw your dirty costume into her grill and yell, "Light starch!"

c. Immediately punch up imdb.com and log in her latest role as "the loser."

2. You studied all weekend for a math test, and when you get your grade, you discover that your best

friend, who hardly ever hits the books, scored better than you. How do you handle it?

a. Congratulate her on a job well done and tell her you'll buy her a soda.

b. Pop the tires on her bike and leave a note that reads, "Can math help you now?"

c. Do research on the Internet into experimental brain-wiping techniques developed by the CIA that you can use to make your friend forget everything she ever knew about fractions and equations.

3. When you hear your parents praising a sibling, what emotion do you feel?

a. Pride. When one member of the family does well, we all do well.

b. A slow, creeping anger. *I can do whatever they did, only better.*

c. What was the question? I'm suddenly seeing only spots, and I'm starting to sweat, shake, and feel light-headed. . . .

4. You've secretly had a crush that you never did anything about, but suddenly you find out the guy's dating your younger sister. What do you do?

a. Tell yourself your sister had no idea about your crush and find another guy to date.

b. Start leaving really lame New Kids on the Block and Jennifer Love Hewitt CDs around your sister's room in hopes he'll break up with her.

c. Secretly steal your sister's identity by wearing her clothes and getting a new haircut, then steal her boyfriend, just like in that really bad Josh Hartnett movie.

5. In any given week, how often would you say you become jealous?
   a. Pretty much never. I'm cool like dat.
   b. Definitely no more than once or twice a day.
   c. How many minutes are there in a week again?

6. You show up at the school dance, only to find that your archrival is wearing the hot dress you really wanted but your parents refused to buy for you. What's next?
   a. What's the big deal? We both look hot.
   b. Surreptitiously affix a fake price tag to the back of her dress that says $9.99.
   c. Keep pointing to something imaginary on the floor so she'll bend over and everyone at the dance will see from the lines that she's wearing granny panties.

7. Even though you've started as sweeper on the soccer team for two straight years, the coach decides to start someone else. You conclude he:
   a. Is just doing his job. Maybe the other girl is playing better right now.
   b. Must have it in for you. He's hated you ever since you laughed in sex ed class when he tried to put a condom on a banana, unsuccessfully.

c. Is secretly in love with the other player's mother and will do anything to win her favor.

8. When you take quizzes like this in books and magazines, you:
a. Share your answers and have a laugh with friends.
b. Keep the answers to yourself for fear that your friends might have scored higher
c. Why are you asking me this, you creep? Who are you going to tell about my score? I didn't do that badly, and really, I totally wasn't trying.

Scoring:
If you answered "a" most of the time, you are a completely cool person who rarely gets jealous and has no need of this book. Now drop it and go see a movie.

If you answered "b" most of the time, you might need help dealing with what your school nurse might politely call issues. Others better hope they never cross you.

If you answered "c" most of the time, you're not someone to be trifled with. Your rampant jealousy would make you the perfect villain on *Desperate Housewives*. Or at least cut out to run for Congress.

CONFESSIONS OF A JEALOUS GIRL
Susan Juby

The first time I felt jealous was when I realized there was a difference between my family and those families I came to think of as ski people.

Ski people drove Volvos with skis tied to the top. Ski children got good grades. Everyone in a ski family had blond hair and was taller than average. They were healthy and vigorous and vaguely Scandinavian. This was in contrast to my family. We were just vague. My mother drove an orange Lada, which was, to my mind (and probably the automakers'), a cheap and pathetic imitation of a Volvo. We didn't ski. Instead we kept chickens. Not a lot, but enough so you'd notice. That made us chicken people. What was worse, those chickens weren't just for rustic effect. We actually ate them. My stepdad killed them himself.

When I was very young, I didn't know enough to be embarrassed by this. In fact, my older brother and I even had this game in which we took bets on how far the chickens would run after they'd had their heads cut off. I have this indelible image, accurate or not, of us watching some unfortunate hen sprinting, headless, across the pasture and me looking up to see a Volvo full of ski people passing, watching us. I could practically hear them saying over the hum of the

German-engineered motor, "Look, Svend, look at those chicken children!"

As I grew older I graduated from being jealous of ski people to being jealous of anyone more fortunate than me in *any conceivable* area. Self-consciousness descended like an ax and I began to resent nearly everyone, including girls whose hair feathered better than mine, girls whose parents took them on holidays to warm places, girls who got new clothes (even ugly clothes), and girls who had better-shaped eyes than mine. This last area was of particular concern to me. I liked an almond-shaped eye and thought that my whole life would be better if my eyes were just slightly less round. I felt that my puffy postsleep eyes were headed in the right direction, and I tried to train them to stay in that shape through excessive sleeping and salt consumption, but with poor results.

About the time I discovered boys, I also discovered that I had a gift for getting into trouble. Soon, I was a genuine problem child—smoking, skipping school, and hanging around places I wasn't supposed to. My new lifestyle ensured that I did not mature at a normal pace. Instead of becoming more comfortable with myself and my place in the world, I grew more and more uncertain and insecure. And much, much more jealous.

Have you ever wondered what those bitter-looking girls wearing too much eyeliner who hang around smoking sullenly on street corners are thinking? I can tell you through personal experience. They are basically thinking, "I hate you," as well as "I wish I was you."

As my friends and I got more and more into doing things I'm not about to discuss for fear of reprisal, all those parts of us that should have been filled with self-esteem came to be filled with bitter resentment. We battered each other with our jealousy, particularly when it came to competing for the affections of boys.

Romantic jealousy was a whole category unto itself that seemed more serious than our usual envy and insecurity, and also more justified. "Did that cow look at him? She better not look at him because *I will end her!*" This from the mellowest girl in our class. Then there was the jealousy aimed at the guy himself. "Are you looking at her? You better not be looking at her or she will be the last thing you ever see." This was voiced by a teacher to her boyfriend. Even though romantic jealousy had a pathological, murderous quality, at least within our group we had a set of rules to help us cope with it. You didn't flirt with or look at your friend's boyfriend. You didn't date your friend's ex-boyfriend, even if they'd been broken up for over a week. If some girl from outside the group threatened your friend's relationship, you turned on the offender *en masse* like a cackling pack of demented hyenas. We knew how it was supposed to work.

Most people will admit to being jealous in love, but almost nobody will admit to feeling jealous about anything else. I'd say my friends and I spent at least a third of our time cutting each other down to size, a third of our time being jealous about boys, and a third of our time resenting "nice girls." Our main after-school activity, besides smoking and looking as bored as possible, was directing ill will at the clean-cut girls with good grades who participated in intramural sports and other teacher-sanctioned after-school activities. God help them if they were rich, too.

My friends, who were only slightly less psychotically jealous than me, coined a name for these smart, nice, well-adjusted girls. We called them Bubblegummers.

I can't remember whether the term was meant to convey some sticking-to-the-shoe type quality, or was a reference to the way that nice girls were shiny and sweet and stuck together (a smart move given the resentment we trained on them). Either way, it was not a compliment.

We spent hours, days, weeks disliking those Bubblegummers. Every time one would casually mention something she'd read in *Time* magazine, we would roll our eyes to show that we were sickened by her pretentiousness. (I did this, in spite of the fact that I was a closet reader who had to dumb down my own vocabulary so my friends wouldn't roll their eyes at *me*.) The Bubblegummers were what was wrong with the world. My friends and I wouldn't look half so sullen and trashy if the Bubblegummers would just stop showing up for class and combing their hair!

Fortunately, the Bubblegummers had enough sense and taste to avoid "our" men, or the situation might have grown serious.

It was actually a girl whom I would have considered a Bubblegummer who finally got me to take a look at my jealousy. A year after high school I worked at a wilderness lodge as a housekeeper/waitress. The job was hard. Sometimes it felt like being in a prison, but with killer sunsets. We were up at five-thirty and worked until seven-thirty at night, seven days a week, for two and a half months.

Five us of worked there: two guides, two housekeepers, and one cook. My partner at the lodge, to my dismay, was perhaps the most perfect girl in the world. Seriously. She had been asked to model multiple times but turned down the opportunity out of some kind of (in my eyes) misguided humility. Her parents were a doctor and a diplomat. She was a Quaker, for god's sake. A vegetarian. She was the hardest worker I have ever met. She was also frugal. And she had this collection of long skirts and blouses that she wore when it was her night to serve the guests dinner. It was the Prada of wilderness lodge wear, particularly when compared to my outfits: short skirts, tights, big black shoes—stuff that played well on Queen Street in Toronto, but looked terrible in a rustic setting.

And worst of all, my partner, "Joan," was nice. I'm not talking garden-variety nice, I mean the kind of nice only ever witnessed before on *Little House on the*

Prairie. She was kind, thoughtful, and considerate, and for some unfathomable reason, she thought I was great. Anyone else would have pegged me as insecure from a mile away. Not Joan. She trusted me.

The minute I laid eyes on her I knew we were in for trouble. She was so tall and healthy. Her skin glowed. The girl was radiant. I, meanwhile, felt furtive, stunted, and pasty from years of my unhealthy lifestyle.

As I said, Joan was a good worker. No, make that a *fantastic* worker. And she was an object of affection for the wealthy and, often as not, elderly guests. She was like a favored granddaughter. The cook liked her and the boss *loved* her. Joan was his kind of employee: hardworking and physically flawless, with a fantastic can-do attitude. The less said about me and my attitude, the better.

As I felt myself growing more and more jealous of Joan, I tried to tell myself that she wasn't perfect. For instance, she was clumsy. She had an accident at least once a day. The problem was partly enthusiasm. She was so eager that she charged right into all kinds of hazards. Her height made her stumbles impressive: they had the grandeur of a falling tree. She always laughed good-naturedly, adding yet another Band-Aid to a freshly bloodied palm or scraped knee. I laughed too, somewhat less good-naturedly.

I didn't want to be jealous. I could appreciate Joan from an outsider's perspective. She was terrific. So every time anyone expressed their admiration for her, and I felt jealous, it made me feel like a snake. "Why don't they say that about me?" was my interior refrain, followed by: "Why am I so awful and insecure?"

I cringe to admit it, but I began to obsess about terrible things happening to Joan. I would take my lunch out in the boat and float in the middle of the lake, dreaming of ways she might disappear. I imagined her falling into the lake and drowning, getting lost in the bush and never coming back, bonking her head in one of her many falls and going into a coma. It wasn't that I didn't like her; I just couldn't stand the way she made me feel. And the more I hated having her around, the more I realized what a terrible person I'd become: neurotic, insecure and, worst of all, jealous.

My resentment toward Joan began to leak out. Sharp words escaped me like needles piercing a bag. She was such an innocent, she had no idea how to react. She had not yet learned the defenses used by perfect girls against the mundane spite of those less perfect. Soon the atmosphere around the camp was poisoned with gossip and hurt feelings.

The more negative energy swirled around, the worse things got. People started taking sides. It was a mess. Was all this the fault of my jealousy? Had I turned what had at first been a certain camaraderie into a seething pit of competition and hostility? I felt like something trapped in a toilet, swirling in a bowl of envy, anger, and resentment: buffeted and bashed, rushing ever downward.

By the time the summer ended I was thoroughly disgusted with myself. I had destroyed the experience with my jealousy. Not only that, but Joan had wised up to me. Away from the job and back in the city, I realized that she could have been a very good friend. But she would never trust me again. It was enough to make me take a long look at myself. I had to do something about the envy, resentment, ill will, bitterness, covetousness, distrust, doubt, and insecurity that were messing up my life. I wanted to be rid of them all.

The mere decision to change didn't cure me of being jealous. That took a lot of work on my self-esteem and a life based on more than pretense. The opposites of jealousy are generosity and trust; both qualities Joan had in abundance. I had to open up to see other people's excellence as more than a commentary on myself. If I worked with Joan today, I know I'd be able to appreciate her for the great person she is.

Sure, I still experience the odd pang of envy. Something about Gwyneth Paltrow can bring it on again, as can any discussion of Jennifer Aniston's hair. But envying celebrities is like wanting to *become* Malibu Barbie. Even I know it is ridiculous.

Sometimes I think about that little chicken child that I used to be, standing in the pasture watching the ski people drive by in their Volvos, and I think I can even appreciate *her* now. Sure, her family had entirely too many chickens. But she was her own person, and that's worth something.

WE'RE ALL GREEN ABOUT SOMETHING
Kristina Bauman and Christian Bauman

Eric fumbled for a cigarette, all backed up against a brick warehouse, chalky red and sprinkled with graffiti and wads of bubble gum. He pulled the last Marlboro from the pocket of his bomber jacket and struck a match off the bricks, then brought it up to the end of the cigarette. Flicking his wrist, he sailed the burning match over the sidewalk and toward the curb where it sizzled into an oil-streaked puddle.

He hung the cigarette crooked from the corner of his mouth and walked, farther into the dark of the city, hands shoved in his pockets.

When he got to her building, he tilted his head back to look at the smoke-stained sky. Eric stared, sighed, then returned his gaze to Earth—the set of steel stairs and thin railing that accompanied it, leading up to a matching steel door. Pulling a final drag from his smoke, Eric tossed the butt to the ground, stepping on it as he walked up the stairs and leaned on the buzzer.

A muffled voice filtered out through the screened-in speaker to the side of the door. "Who is it?"

"Eric."

"Damn it, okay, hold on."

He heard bolts slide; then the heavy door swung in. A silhouette of a woman stood in the dark opening.

"What the hell do you want?" the woman asked, not moving from her spot.

"Hey, Luce," Eric said. He tried a grin. She didn't see or didn't care. The woman stood silent. Finally, though, she stepped backward, holding the door open.

"Come on."

Eric walked in, letting Lucy shut the door behind him and slide the bolts into place. She climbed the stairs behind the door, talking over her shoulder as they went.

"So what is it now?"

"Come on, what do you think it is?"

"You want your money, right?" she asked, rounding the first corner and going up the next flight.

"Yeah, I want my money. It's been two months. I can't just let this slide."

"I know, I know. I've got it . . . it's upstairs."

Eric followed in silence as Lucy led him to the third floor. She pulled a key out of the pocket of her ratty purple sweater and unlocked the stained brown door, leading him in, slamming the door behind her. Eric stood by the door as she disappeared into the next room, mumbling something under her breath. He heard another door slam and guessed she was in the bathroom. He leaned against the door, grinding his teeth, staring at the ceiling.

Richard's fingers paused on the keyboard as he reread his words on the computer screen. Like they were glued, the pads of his fingers. Resting on the last four letters of the last word he'd typed—three fingers from his right hand on "L," "I," "N," and his left index finger on "G." He leaned forward, reading it all again: . . . *grinding his teeth, staring at the ceiling.* Satisfied, Richard let his breath out and lifted his fingers from the keys. He saved his work, backed it up on a CD, pushed his chair away from the tiny desk. He popped his jaw, then released the CD from the computer and played with it in his hands. Richard stared, absently running a palm over his pimpled cheek, then through his long black hair. He stared, then slowly, slowly, began to smile.

This is it, he thought, and his smile grew wider. He'd never written better.

His bedroom was dark. From down the hall he could hear his father snoring. Seemed lately he did nothing but snore. Sleep and snore alone in his bedroom, the phone ringing unanswered all day, Richard either at school or up here typing, his father snoring through it all.

But whatever. Richard looked down at the CD in his hand.

It was funny, in a way. To feel so good. Because writing wasn't, always. Good, that is. It went well. Almost always. But the place he wrote from, the place in his head . . .

Like this Eric, for instance.

Eric was . . .

Richard snorted, running his fingertips along the edges of the disk.

Eric was sort of what Richard might like to be. Well, not exactly *be*, mind you. But the spirit of him. The . . . the *flavor*.

"I'd like a new flavor," Richard said aloud, and his voice in the dark bedroom almost scared him—but then he snorted again and laughed. "I *would* like a new flavor."

Maybe high school would be easier with a new flavor. If he was more like Eric, well, then . . .

Richard laughed to himself. Who cares. School was a slow, burning torture, but who cares. This CD was the ticket beyond all that.

Fat Frank heard the sound of footsteps in the hall. Blanket to double chin, he lay without moving, listening to the sounds of his son moving through the house. Toilet flushing. The creak on the top stair, then the creak on the one in the middle. A pause. Then the front door swinging shut. Click. Fat Frank didn't move. He listened. Nothing else. Alone in the dark he breathed out hard then pushed the covers back, swinging his legs to the floor.

He hadn't always been Fat Frank. Once he'd been Furious Frank. Furious Frank Corbo. Literary icon. Definer of his generation. Prose for his people, he called it. Righting the wrongs in words. A trim, lean fighter in a double-breasted suit, the two-word head-line centered under his photo on the cover of *Time* magazine: Furious Frank.

He wasn't furious anymore. He was tired. He pulled his bathrobe on, crossing it over his belly, tying it best he could. He was tired. He was fat. Fat Frank. Fat Frank Corbo. He rubbed his jaw and left the room, first time in two days.

Frank paused at the top of the stairs. He'd been planning on going down, to get something to eat. But he changed his mind. Instead he shuffled down the hall to the boy's room. He knocked on the door, even though he'd heard him leave with his own ears. Still, you never know. He knocked. No answer. Frank reached for the handle, pushed the door open.

The bedroom was dark, with a green glow from the corner. The boy's computer monitor, left on. The boy fancied himself a writer. Fat Frank tried not to get involved.

The therapist they'd gone to twice after Fat Frank's wife died—this was three years ago, and although no longer Fighting, Frank wasn't quite Fat yet—had thought the boy's writing hobby to be an issue between them. "He's jealous of you, Frank. He's a little boy looking up at a big mountain."

Fat Frank thought it ridiculous. Although, three years later, the big mountain part wasn't far off. He rubbed an open hand over his bathrobed belly. Big mountain, indeed.

And jealousy—what was that, anyway? A vague thing. In the corner, the boy's computer monitor glowed green. *We're all green about something,* Fat Frank thought.

He turned back to the hall, then changed his mind again and stepped into the boy's room. Pushed through piles of clothes, potato chip bags, issues of *Rolling Stone,* to the desk in the corner. Fat Frank sat down hard on the boy's little chair. It squeaked, but held him. He blinked, adjusting his eyes, then focused on the screen.

Eric stood by the door as she disappeared into the next room, mumbling something under her breath. He heard another door slam and guessed she was in the bathroom. He leaned against the door, grinding his teeth, staring at the ceiling.

Frank sniffed, wiped his nose. Allergies. He put a finger out, hesitated, then pressed the up arrow. The text scrolled up. And up. And up.

"Boy's been busy," he said aloud. He got to the top, hesitated again, then began reading.

It took almost an hour to read it all. And when he was done Fat Frank went back to the top and read it again. And then he sat—alone in the dark, on his son's chair, at his son's desk, at the foot of his son's creation—for a long time. He didn't move until he heard the front door open and slam and then footsteps coming up the stairs. He turned his head to look at the bedroom door as Richard appeared in the doorway.

His son's eyes stared silently at his father as Fat Frank pulled his bulk from the seat and Richard moved into the room, wordless.

Fat Frank dropped his gaze. *Yeah, we're all green about something,* he thought. *Isn't that the truth.*

TŒ THE LINE WITH ME
Matthea Harvey

We needed water & frozen water
for the party. I chose you to two-step

with but the downstairs chandelier
stayed still, its prisms prim.

Consider this: if sunfish
& ducks compete for the same bit

of bread, at any moment their mouths
might meet. That's how my mother

explained the Other, told me to hedge
my bets, furl wish-scrolls into

the topiary. Still I had questions
about Life & the Afterlife. You

looked in through the screen door.
I sat next to my ex.

ALL JEALOUSY, ALL THE TIME:
Extras

JEALOUSY VS. ENVY: IMPRESS YOUR ENGLISH TEACHER

Jealous: 1.Resentful and envious, as of someone's success, advantages, etc. 2.Proceeding from suspicious fears or envious resentment. 3.Inclined to suspicions of rivalry, unfaithfulness, etc., as in love.

Envy: 1. A feeling of resentful discontent, begrudging admiration, or covetousness with regard to another's advantages, possessions, or attainments; desire for something possessed by another.

(Definitions from *Random House Webster's College Dictionary*)

BEING WELL-READ MAKES SOME PEOPLE JEALOUS

An assortment of picture books, novels, nonfiction, and online essays about our favorite topic.

The Berenstain Bears and the Green-Eyed Monster, Stan and Jan Berenstain (Random House, 1995): Are bears afraid of monsters?

The English Roses, Madonna (Calloway, 2003): *Mean Girls* for the picture book set from the mother of two.

"Envy," Kathryn Chetkovich (*Granta* 82: Life's Like That: www.granta.com/extracts/2015) (2003): A refreshingly honest personal essay about one writer's envy of her boyfriend, a more successful (and famous) writer.

Envy, Jason Epstein (Oxford University Press, 2003): The New York Public Library asked seven writers to tackle one each of the seven deadly sins (anger, envy, gluttony, greed, lust, pride, and sloth). *Envy* is nonfiction and might feel a bit too much like homework, but it's an interesting overview of everything envy.

Gossip Girl, Cecily Von Ziegesar (Little, Brown, 2002-2006): You know you love this series.

"Our Mutual Friend: How to steal friends and influence people," Lucinda Rosenfeld (*New York Magazine*: newyorkmetro.com/nymetro/shopping/features/9748/) (2004): This is what happens when you introduce two people and they become friends, leaving you behind!

I'm Not Jealous: How to Beat the Mean Greens, Claudine Desmarteau (Universe, 2004): An adorable picture book originally published in France.

Jacob Have I Loved, Katherine Paterson (Harper Trophy, 1980): If you have siblings you'll be able to relate to this classic novel. If you are an only child you will be glad.

Odd Girl Speaks Out: Girls Write about Bullies, Cliques, Popularity, and Jealousy, Rachel Simmons (Harvest Books, 2004): Letters, essays, and poems submitted by real girls.

Othello, William Shakespeare (c. 1604): This is the one where the character Iago calls jealousy a green-ey'd monster. And he should know.

Spilling Open: The Art of Becoming Yourself, Sabrina Ward Harrison (Villard, 2000): This gorgeous book will inspire you to write and paint and let go of your insecurities.

MAKE YOUR OWN JEALOUSY MIX!

"Hey Jealousy" (Gin Blossoms, *New Miserable Experience*)

"Mr. Brightside" (The Killers, *Hot Fuss*)

"Jealous Guy" (John Lennon, *Imagine*)

"Why Can't I Be You" (The Cure, *Kiss Me, Kiss Me, Kiss Me*)

"Jealousy" (Natalie Merchant, *Tigerlily*)

"Circus Envy" (REM, *Monster*)

"We Hate It When Our Friends Become Successful" (Morrissey, *Your Arsenal*)

"Jealousy" (Liz Phair, *Whip-Smart*)

"I'm Jealous" (Ike and Tina Turner, *The Soul of Ike and Tina Turner*)

"Jealousy" (Pet Shop Boys, *Behavior*)

"So Jealous" (Tegan and Sara, *So Jealous*)

"Bein' Green" (Kermit the Frog, *The Muppet Show: Music, Mayhem, And More! The 25th Anniversary Collection*)

GREEN-EYED VIEWING

(A partial, PG-13 version. You've seen all the R ones already, anyway.)

Addams Family Values (1993)
Directed by Barry Sonnenfeld. Starring Anjelica Huston, Raul Julia, Christina Ricci, and Joan Cusack.
Wednesday (Ricci) and Pugsley try to kill their new brother, Pubert, which leads to the hiring of a new nanny (Cusack), which leads to trouble.

Amadeus (1984)
Directed by Milos Forman. Starring F. Murray Abraham and Tom Hulce.
Who knew classical music could be so competitive? The story of Mozart (Hulce), as told by his biggest rival (Abraham). Best Picture Academy Award Winner.

Envy (2004)
Directed by Barry Levinson. Starring Ben Stiller and Jack Black.
The explanation for this mediocre movie about a friendship torn apart by envy? It sat on a shelf, unreleased, until Mr. Black hit it big with *School of Rock* (2003). You'll see why if you actually rent it.

Ever After (1998)

Directed by Andy Tennant. Starring Drew Barrymore, Anjelica Huston, and Dougray Scott.

One word: stepsisters. A live-action update of Cinderella. (As opposed to the 1950 Disney animated one.)

Love and Basketball (2000)

Directed by Gina Prince-Bythewood. Starring Sanaa Lathan, Omar Epps, Alfre Woodard, and Dennis Haysbert.

Set in the pre-WNBA basketball world of the 1980s, when the options for a girl with game were limited.

Mean Girls (2004)

Directed by Mark S. Waters. Starring Lindsay Lohan, Rachel McAdams, and Tina Fey.

"I'm sorry that people are so jealous of me . . . but I can't help it that I'm so popular."—Gretchen. If you must, also see Lindsay's "song," "First," from her "album," *Speak*.

My Best Friend's Wedding (1997)

Directed by P. J. Hogan. Starring Julia Roberts, Dermot Mulroney, Cameron Diaz, and Rupert Everett.

What does Julia have to be jealous about? Rupert was the only option here.

"The One with All the Jealousy": *Friends,* Episode 3.12 (Season Three, 1997)

Ross + Rachel = Jealousy.

Real Women Have Curves (2002)

Directed by Patricia Cardoso. Starring America Ferrara and Lupe Ontiveros.

Ana (Ferrara) must choose between her family's expectations, fueled, in part, by her mother's jealousy, and her dreams. Winner of the Audience Award at the 2002 Sundance Film Festival.

School Ties (1992)

Directed by Robert Mandel. Starring Brendan Fraser, Matt Damon, Chris O'Donnell, and Ben Affleck.

When David Green (Fraser) is recruited to play football his senior year at a Massachusetts prep school and takes Charlie Dillon's (Damon) position on the team *and* his girlfriend, Dillon's jealousy turns ugly.

Snow White and the Seven Dwarfs (1937)

Starring (voices) Adriana Caselotti, Harry Stockwell, Roy Atwell, and Lucille La Verne.

Who is the fairest of them all? Don't answer that.

Toy Story (1995)

Directed by John Lasseter. Starring (voices) Tom Hanks and Tim Allen.

Personally, I prefer Mr. Potato Head (Don Rickles) to either Woody (Hanks) or Buzz Lightyear (Allen).

BUY GREEN!

Fragrance: Sephora.com says Envy (Gucci) is "a transparent floral fragrance" and Envy Me (Gucci) "was created for the woman who demands attention." Hmm.

Tea: Envy (Tazo: www.tazo.com)
Described as "a floral, somewhat nutty blend of organic green teas from the misty mountains of Southwestern China." "Nutty" seems to be the important word here.

IT'S NOT THAT EASY BEIN' GRANNY SMITH APPLE:
Crayola's Twenty Shades of Green

(Hopefully, your jealousy green isn't Shadow. Or Inch Worm . . .)

Asparagus
Caribbean Green
Electric Lime
Fern
Forest Green
Granny Smith Apple
Green
Green Yellow
Inch Worm
Jungle Green
Mountain Meadow
Olive Green
Pine Green
Screamin Green
Sea Green
Shadow
Shamrock
Spring Green
Tropical Rain Forest
Yellow Green

Capricorns (Dec. 22–Jan. 19)
are known for being jealous.

ABOUT THE CONTRIBUTORS

SIOBHAN ADCOCK was born in the Chicago area and is the author of *30 Things Everyone Should Know How to Do Before Turning 30,* a bossy instruction manual. She teaches creative writing and creative nonfiction in New York state.

What she's most jealous of: "I am a jealous, mean, covetous person, so the sad truth is that I am envious of just about everybody: snowboarders, musicians, surfers, people with curly hair . . . But I suppose I'm most jealous of people who can drive stick shift. People who drive stick like to brag about how fun it is. It probably is really fun. Jerks."

E. LOCKHART is the author of *The Boyfriend List* and its forthcoming sequel, *The Boy Book*—both of which feature Ruby Oliver and Tate Prep. She also wrote *Fly on the Wall,* and can be found at www.the boyfriendlist.com. She actually likes to bake.

What she's most jealous of: "I envy talents I don't have: facility with foreign languages, hand-eye coordination, beautiful singing voices, speed."

ANNELI RUFUS is the author of several books, including *Party of One: The Loner's Manifesto*. Thus she is largely reclusive, but she can be lured into conversation if the topic is sharks, ghosts, or the Wild West.

What she's most jealous of: "Girls with beautiful hair, and everyone with beach houses."

THATCHER HELDRING grew up in Seattle and went to the University of Washington. After college he sold his car and moved to New York, where he presently lives and writes. He is happily engaged and looks forward to being married sometime in the postponable future.

What he's most jealous of: "People who speak more than one language and have never heard of Ashlee Simpson."

NED VIZZINI is the author of *Be More Chill* (Hyperion/Miramax Books), chosen by Judy Blume as a *Today* show Book Club selection, and *Teen Angst? Naaah…* (Free Spirit), published when the author was nineteen. His work has received awards from New York Is Book Country, Book Sense, and the New York Public Library. Ned's new book, *It's Kind of a Funny Story,* is slated for publication by Hyperion/Miramax Books in spring 2006. Ned lives in Brooklyn, New York. You can find him at NedVizzini.com.

What he's most jealous of: "I'm most jealous of

women I see on television—or the men with these women. This is why I try and watch for a maximum of fifteen minutes at once, unless I have a friend to guide me."

MARTY BECKERMAN is the sexy and delicate twenty-two-year-old author of the modern-day classics *Death to All Cheerleaders* (Infected Press, 2000), *Generation S.L.U.T.* (MTV Books, 2004), and the forthcoming *Retard Nation* (Simon & Schuster, 2006). A recent honors graduate of American University, Beckerman lives in Washington, D.C. His Web site is www.MartyBeckerman.com.

What he's most jealous of: "My friend Ned Vizzini, for his endless charisma, luscious girlfriends, and freakin' Enormous _____."

JACLYN MORIARTY grew up in Sydney and studied law in England and the United States. She is the author of the internationally bestselling *Feeling Sorry for Celia* and *The Year of Secret Assignments*. Her first adult novel, *I Have a Bed Made of Buttermilk Pancakes*, was published by Anansi Press, Canada, in August 2005. She has worked as a media and entertainment lawyer in Sydney but now lives in Montreal, where she writes full-time.

What she's most jealous of: "I'm jalous of people who can spell."

DYAN SHELDON was born in Brooklyn but now lives in London. She is the author of several novels, including *Confessions of a Teenage Drama Queen.*

What she's most jealous of: "I don't know about jealous, but I am rather envious of my friend Alison. Partly because Alison worked on *The Sopranos.* Partly because, having worked on *The Sopranos,* she got to know Steve van Zandt and has been invited backstage at a gig to meet Bruce Springsteen and the E Street Band. But mainly because Alison lives with Roxie the pit bull, who is undeniably the greatest dog in Brooklyn, if not the whole world. I would love to call Roxie my dog."

IRINA REYN was born in Moscow and arrived in the United States at the age of seven. The trials and tribulations of her immigrant experience have been chronicled in the anthology *Becoming American: Personal Essays by First Generation Immigrant Women* (Hyperion). Since then, Irina has been an editor of the online magazine *Killing the Buddha*, a (jealous) book reviewer, and a teacher of creative writing. She is working on her first novel, along with a collection of short stories.

What she's most jealous of: "Believe it or not, I am most jealous of anyone going back to school in September. I wish I could be a student again, with my overstuffed book bag, late-night dorm chats and pizza deliveries to look forward to, but with no pressing need to decide what I will do with the rest of my life."

REED TUCKER lives in a cold, dark room somewhere in New York City, where he sits around wishing he had Donald Trump's money, President Bush's power, and above all, Usher's sweet, sweet dance moves.

What he's most jealous of: "David Moore, a kid I knew in sixth grade whose family was fortunate enough to own a revolutionary technology called a laserdisc player he swore would change the world."

SUSAN JUBY lives on Vancouver Island with her husband, James, and their dog, Frank. She enjoys horseback riding, knitting, and pasta.

What she's most jealous of: Susan is relieved to say that she is no longer a poster child for jealousy. She can still be a bit judgmental, but only when she hasn't eaten.

KRISTINA BAUMAN is a high school senior in New Jersey. She dabbles in photography, writing, and other arts. Her father, **CHRISTIAN BAUMAN**, writes novels and other propaganda. Find out more at www.christian bauman.com.

What they're most jealous of: After some thought and consideration of the world at large, Kristina finds very little to be jealous of. Christian admits a twinge of jealousy of those more thoughtful and considerate than he is.

MATTHEA HARVEY is the author of two books of poetry, *Sad Little Breathing Machine* (Graywolf, 2004) and *Pity the Bathtub Its Forced Embrace of the Human Form* (Alice James Books, 2000). She lives in Brooklyn.

What she's most jealous of: "I am jealous of detectives and people who have more than one dachshund."

ABOUT THE EDITOR

MARISSA WALSH lives in Queens but she's sure the grass is greener in Brooklyn.

What she's most jealous of: "Well, if you read the introduction, you know that I'm jealous of just about everything. But the *first* time I remember being jealous—insanely, sobbingly jealous—was after reading *Charlotte's Web*. I desperately wanted to trade places with Fern, to be Fern. I didn't want to live in the city—I wanted to live on a farm, and I wanted a cute, cuddly pig (remember that picture in the book of Fern cradling Wilbur in her arms like a little baby doll?) to call my own, and I wanted to go to the county fair and get stuck on the top of the Ferris wheel with a boy. My mother tried to console me, but she wasn't about to buy me a pig—or send me to live on a farm—so there wasn't much she could do, except try to make me realize what I did have, and why my life was just as good as Fern's. Honestly, she wasn't much help; I had to get over it on my own. And as I got older I realized that, like most things, pigs lose their charm when they grow up."

More jealousy can be found at www.thejealousy book.com.